# When a Phoenix Rose Nevermore

Cycles of the Phoenix II

First edition.

Cover designed by Sabina Kencana.

Edited by Fluky Fiction.

# Cycles of the Phoenix Saga

*Cycles of the Phoenix*

*When a Phoenix Rose Nevermore*

Table of Contents

# Book I

# Goodbye, I Love You

## Dahlia Noelle's Odyssey

# Chapter I

## Worthy

The luminous waters of baby Dahlia's eyes reflected her father's face, as her appearance floated upon his eyes. With the gentleness of a lullaby whose whisper soars upon a breeze for distant souls to meet, Karlo Noelle sang to his newly adopted eight-week-old daughter,

> Worthiness arrives not from victories.
> Nor can it be received from others' praise.
> It is free from Acceptance's decrees.
> You exist; therefore, you are wonderful.

Only a dying echo of frustration fluttered within Karlo's ribs for still not solving the mystery of a non-rhyming conclusion to his song that he prepared for her, even as he perceived that its imperfection fit the message. Yet his vexation was washed over by Dahlia's warmth as he cradled her, her radiant smile, and the irregular beat of her coos that rippled into his chest. Unused to feeling such radiant joy, he roared with laughter. Feeling and seeing this immense symphony from her dad caused a whirlwind of laughter to dance within her, its thunder to flee through her rapturous smile, and its rain to gently fall from her twilight-brown eyes. Karlo slightly raised his head to protect Dahlia's face from being watered by his bliss-fueled tears.

That memory projected itself upon the forefront of his mind when he cradled Dahlia twenty-three years later, as he sobbed, and his tears descended upon his daughter while warmth slowly abandoned her.

# Chapter II

## Happily Ever After

Dr. Jefferson Colm's office window came face-to-face with the new twenty-three-year old client who sat beside it. The windows to Dahlia's soul angled up to the palm fronds which appeared to shyly wave at her in the breeze, as if the shrubs were experiencing an affliction of dejection, loneliness, yearning, and hopefulness, unsure if she would acknowledge them. She perceived this even as most of her mental faculties remained at choosing a response and as she strove to keep death from overtaking her. Her therapist's lack of well-being had been betrayed by the subtle lilt of his voice, the faint tremble of his earnest gaze, and the slightly overcompensating smile that masked his sorrow of a secret origin. Dahlia perceived two enticing paths which she could pursue: one of truth, the other a tale of embellishment that led to a Happily Ever After. She decided to give Dr. Colm hope despite the guilt that gently tugged (like a child persistently and desperately attempting to gain a preoccupied parent's attention about a matter that was important to them, while trying not to be rude) at her heart. Yet she feared that the entity would consume her if she traveled down the other road.

Thus, Dahlia faced Dr. Colm with a smile that was carefully tempoed in its unfolding while she shot her vision diagonally and upwards to her left; she began her construction and presentation of a story nearly simultaneously, so it seemed that she was sharing a memory. She glanced at her therapist as she relayed how her friends frequently made strides to reach out to her, as she did with them; how they strived to include her, as she endeavored to the same; and how they fought to reassure her, as she aspired to. Dahlia could sense relief incrementally wash over Dr. Colm as he nodded in understanding and encouragement; the fringes of the doctor's solace laid a comforting hand on her heart that had felt like it was itching to enter a heavy metal beat when she had chosen to tell a comforting lie.

Dahlia left her appointment with that relentless, ever-evolving, and energy-draining depression that imploded her soul and dully cut her nerves, but imparting sanitized fairy tale-toned vignettes to her college counselor conceived a semblance of giddiness in the heart of her diaphragm and its warmth radiated throughout her chest. The sun appeared to be ever more jolly as its width continued to match the size of its unfolding growth spurt (while its luminous face turned ever more scarlet) when it met the horizon upon its counterclockwise descent.

Dahlia sat on a public bench emblazoned with a delirious-looking indigo praying mantis mascot, and she proceeded with her first therapy assignment: to list catastrophic scenarios that challenged her mental health, describe what the likelihood of those scenarios occurring would be, the worst and best-case outcomes, healthy ways to cope with the crises, and what messages of encouragement would put her mind at ease during these predicaments (or what she would say to a friend who was experiencing them). The sensation of her melancholia persisted, yet it was as if she had finally entered a branching reality where the roles between it and her were reversed; now it was the co-pilot, while she was the captain.

Later on, Dahlia would experience how transferring the foundation of her perceptions on the emotion of this euphoric relief (rather than reaching and maintaining healthy optimism, without emotional reliance) from a depressed and anxious one was even more dangerous than if her discernment remained rooted in the familiar deceptions of melancholia.

Night had solidified by the time Dahlia strolled toward her apartment. The summer breeze briskly tagged and begged her to chase it, persistent yet mindful enough to not proceed beyond a run, as if doing so preserved hope that she would play along, even if reluctantly.

# Chapter III

## Trauma and Reasoning

Dahlia sobbed, yet the genesis of her tears was relief that undulated like warm concentric waves expanding from her bosom, reaching into her arms, clouding her vision, and flowing past her eyes, as it crashed upon the inner walls of her upper body. The sensation of her feet was distant; she felt like she was floating above her legs. She and Lance Corinth held each other in an embrace, and their warmth treated the barrier between their bodies as non-existent. Dahlia savored the heat that radiated through them, and she felt grateful about finally being understood. She always wished for this spiritual experience, even more than making love, yet feared that it was a reality that would only ever exist in her imagination. She had yearned to communicate (even without speaking) in the same language of socialization as others, yet Lance above all, he whom she loved at first sight and only became increasingly attracted to as they occasionally shared experiences with one another.

The bedroom slowly took shape around Dahlia's perception as the dream fled from her, and a locomotive of suicidal impulses blindsided her. She yanked a scream away from her lips as she felt gravity pull her toward the neighborhood train tracks. Dahlia had dealt with suicidal desires before, but she thought that she had annihilated them, and they had never arrived as impulses. She tried to focus on her parents sleeping in the bedroom below as the assault seemed to leave a wound that bled lonely memories and projected futures into the nexus of her contemplation; waves of sorrow persisted to crash onto her, dragging her to shifting sand while her chest flowed down a widening cavity even as she attempted to rise and run to the shore of sanity. Dahlia initially fought with everything she had to not give in, but the demons' lullabies were alluring. She left a note on the kitchen table that read, "I'm sorry. Goodbye, I love you."

Dahlia felt like a passenger in her body as she walked through the frigid and clear January morning, about three hours after midnight. Dahlia strolled through the more hushed and lonelier than normal streets as the visitation of freezing air whistled like a mourning banshee through the stretch of infrastructure that huddled together for a shot at survival. The arctic wind, a disciple of death, rapidly shot flaming bullets through every inch of the pajama and sandal-clad Dahlia as her home seemingly shrank behind her; the fine layer of the prior day's deposit of snow drank the dregs of feeling from her feet. Yet the opportunity to freeze to death didn't satiate her undesired impulse for decapitation. The train crossing was merely a block more away on this deserted street, yet Dahlia's memories and immersive thoughts about her suicide's aftermath defied time. These projections became more tangible, while the sensation of the present was like an unconvincing virtual reality program, though her excruciating depression defiantly refused to ease its torment on her pain receptors.

* * *

Dahlia remembered the first time she met Lance. She was twenty-one years old and in a cozy meeting room during her first day as a Hallelujah Comics writer. Her boss, Joanne Beckheart, talked him up as if he were the most wonderful soul who ever arrived into existence. Apparently he was Joanne's cousin, and she behaved as if her mission was to give Dahlia the security of friendship from her and their team, who had been commissioned to create a life-affirming fantasy compilation series named *How the Phoenix Conquered Death*. Joanne seemingly could perceive Dahlia's long-gestating loneliness despite her gregarious smile whenever she was addressed by someone in the room. To be fair, Dahlia soon realized that she may have been stretching her grin a bit too wide in her attempt to ensure a happy demeanor, as she was still adjusting to her joy dying from malnutrition not too long ago. Exhausted from a sleepless night, she was also unaware that her subconscious was initiating a smile to counteract her restless nerves. Dahlia glanced at the meeting room's window behind her and realized that her grin was quite larger than she had guessed, and she rapidly resumed a conservative smile, though seeing the rapid transformation caused a shot of nervous laughter to launch from her; she covered her mouth quickly, which caused the second laugh to escape through her nose and return as a snort. Right then, Dahlia surreptitiously looked at everyone closely for the first time, and she noticed that one guy looked annoyed, but she was relieved that anyone who laid eyes upon her looked at her with varying degrees of kindness; as she looked more closely at Joanne, she noticed that her demeanor of joy and affection were intermingled with a touch of self-conscious nervousness.

A man walked in approximately five minutes before tardiness and with a "good morning" that felt inviting. Dahlia prayed that he wasn't Lance, even as she yearned for it to be him. She was intimidated and enchanted by his beauty, not only in appearance, but in gait, demeanor, and voice, and a refreshing aspect of an individual that she rarely got wrong on initial observation; Dahlia could feel genuineness radiating from him, a phenomenon she didn't necessarily begrudge anyone from lacking, besides herself (she particularly admired, and saw the authenticity of, individuals who attempted to be genuinely loving even though their feelings for that way of being were lacking for whatever reason). The yearning of Dahlia's heart for the man to be Lance were fulfilled as he sat in the chair between her and Joanne. Dahlia tried to suppress her blush as he formally introduced himself to her, but her cheeks kept getting hotter as she shook his hand, which made her more embarrassed and her face all the redder.

During a co-worker's Valentine's night house party a year later, Dahlia cheered for Lance as his and Justine Basker's lips embraced each other, their tongues presumably caressed one another, and their hands traced the other's back as their arms tenderly pressed their torsos together. For a few months, she had fortified her emotions for when the man she loved and the woman he met at a wanderlust club would officially become a couple (it was difficult to downplay the signs); Dahlia was grateful that her resolve didn't slip when she saw them seal the deal by making out in front of her and the rest of the work family. Dahlia's remaining column of hope to be romantically loved by him gave way in a bone-shaking crash of despondency, but she made sure to whoop as loud as she could for them. She prayed her tears were interpreted as joy.

Later that night, Dahlia adjusted and caressed herself in front of her bedroom mirror as she thought about Lance. She closed her eyes and visualized his unclothed body pressed up against hers as their heartbeats and voices intermingled.

Their fingertips slowly skated across the other's, as well as one another's necks, chests, lower backs, derrieres, and inner thighs. When their lips weren't interlocked (nor the tips of their tongues delicately rubbing and tasting one another) they gazed into the other's eyes (which appeared like a twin set of perpetually eclipsed stars that became entranced when they came face to face with another), or they journeyed across the other's body through sight.

Their hands eventually circled their way to the thick curls of hair below their belly buttons, and they continued to progress down below, until they were slowly stroking and rubbing the most erogenous places of one other.

Beads of sweat formed upon Dahlia and Lance, with the appearance of morning dew, before they walked to their bed with held hands. Moving in opposite directions, they led their kisses down the routes where their hands had traversed, their fingers continuing to fondle their lover's body.

Dahlia and Lance faced one another again; they held one another and rhythmically rocked in their final act of lovemaking, but guilt detonated within Dahlia right after she crested the first wave of euphoria.

Dahlia's shame leaked into the epilogue of her routine love making fantasies with Lance, where she cuddled and conversed with him post-coitus.

Dahlia whispered an apology to him and his girlfriend.

Dahlia had fallen platonically in love with Justine (as she did with many souls), so she especially hated the jealousy that instantly sprouted within her when she noticed the romance that blossomed between her and Lance. Dahlia and Justine immediately hit it off, or so Dahlia wished. They complemented one another, but where many of their interests aligned, Dahlia still struggled to communicate, which caused her to feel alone among people whom she loved.

For as long as Dahlia could recall, engaging in conversations was like trying to learn how to master an ever-evolving dance with virtuosos, being thrown into an advanced math class where the rules kept shifting, or attempting fluency in a language whose identity was impossible. Though her understanding of individuals was heightened, her attempt to contribute to conversations felt like locating and reuniting every tiny far-fled shard from a glass figurine; time was expensive, concentration was quick-burning, and accuracy was elusive for this endeavor. Justine also appeared to be lovely in Dahlia's eyes, and she recalled the first time she felt humiliated about her appearance.

Dahlia had tried out for the track team during her senior year at Telton Oak High School, and she was accepted. She had braved this decision because she yearned to belong, and she loved the sensation of flight that running provided, as well as the catharsis she felt from making the world race away from her. The well-established group of friends had never treated her poorly up to this point, but they kept her at acquaintanceship's length despite her efforts to be their friend. However, on this particular day, they had invited her to join them for lunch underneath the oak tree at the school's edge.

They were already there when Dahlia arrived, and she received a chilling electric buzz of foreboding when she noticed that most of them perfunctorily hid their snickers when they saw her amid the silence and glances of pity from the rest of the group.

She didn't hear what they had been talking about, but she attributed her apprehension to misreading them due to her doubts about finally being accepted in their clique. They didn't say anything beyond the pleasantries as Dahlia started to eat her lunch; they were nearly done with theirs. When the others finished eating, Letty Tate (the most popular girl of the widely admired group) asked Dahlia why she refused to wash herself in the public school showers after running like they did and why she changed into her track clothes before team meets, rather than in the locker room with them.

Before Dahlia had time to formulate a response, Letty asked, "What are you, a lesbian?" Some of her friends laughed as Dahlia denied she was, and she nervously stood up to leave.

"Relax, I was joking," Letty replied as she rose, and the others casually stood up and shielded them from view. "Of course you're not into women. Otherwise, you'd be in the locker room enjoying the view every chance you got."

*What an idiotic concept*, Dahlia thought, while she received stress over harming her chance at acceptance with them (even as she wanted nothing to do with them at this point).

Letty was seemingly blind to the rage in Dahlia's eyes, and she felt entitled to probe further when she noticed the fear within them. She inquired, "Me and the girls were talking, and we think we figured it out. You're ashamed because you don't shave down there, do you? You know what we mean; you let your pubes grow, and you probably let them grow wild."

Dahlia's cheeks went scarlet as she looked at the ground and stammered that it wasn't true, but her reaction convinced them otherwise.

Letty, with a smile, told the others who laughed to quiet down, as if she was deaf to their titters up to this point and hadn't been one of the ones who engaged in it (half-suppressed though hers was). She even had the delusion of providing sage advice as she placed a hand on Dahlia's shoulder, and the nerve to literally look down at her with superficial empathy, by telling her that men liked bare women and guys would find her more attractive if she at least trimmed her pubes a little bit. Dahlia responded, "I didn't know that your boyfriend wanted to fuck prepubescent girls, you towering, hairless child."

Regret flowed with Dahlia's words, since she didn't think it was one of her finer retorts (despite a couple of the girls' chuckles). She felt guilty about lobbing an insult at anyone, and for retaliating in a vulnerable situation. She could feel rage and embarrassment poison Letty's sympathetic yet egotistical emotions. Still, Dahlia failed to completely contain a grand laugh, which only inspired the self-appointed guru to appear angrier, yet funnier, in her accompanying confusion. This only helped to tickle Dahlia into another semi-suppressed guffaw, though the burden of her reply, the static of nervous energy from their teammates, and her embarrassment of how she appeared instigated the majority of her stumble into anesthetic laughter. Shock, agony, and terror suddenly consumed her emotions; Letty had slammed her into the tree and was choking her.

Dahlia was released a few seconds later as horror and shame dawned on Letty. She collapsed as she gasped and retched.

Dahlia desperately reasoned that someone would have overcome their shock and helped her if the attack lasted longer, though she feared the assault was a delight for perverse spectation. Still, all the teammates except Letty checked on her, with some voicing their concern, and some even reprimanding Letty. Yet their expressions were intermingled with fear of getting into trouble as they looked around. Her teammates left uncertainly when she asserted that she was okay and that she wouldn't tell on them.

When Dahlia got home, she turned her bathroom faucet as far in the red as possible in an attempt to distract herself from the gaping wound in her soul. Her sobs were drowned by the thunder of the quickly blistering shower, and her tears flowed with the fresh water upon her reddening skin as the invisible agony persisted.

Dahlia's subconscious had buried that memory in its realm a few days later, so she was caught off guard when her reasoning received soon after that the individuals who she loved wanted her dead; she even instinctively felt as if her beverages, if left unattended for even one second, would be poisoned by her loved ones. Dahlia knew these thoughts were beyond the grasp of logic, but they were relentless as they kidnapped her empathy. Compelled by an innate, unconscious desire to survive, she was invaded by thoughts to kill some of them. The compassion and attempts at inclusion from some of her senior classmates (outside of the track team that she had stopped showing up to) flickered to annoyance and malice in her eyes; even though she could objectively separate reality from deception, her emotions felt more persuasive.

Dahlia felt her grasp on reality continue to slip, so over the next six months, she pushed back with every ounce of strength she had to wrench those terrifying thoughts and emotions around to aim at her, locking them in place; she made such a habit of laying blame for interpersonal mistakes upon herself (even in the instances where she was innocent), psychologically abusing herself, and finding the beauty of others' humanity no matter what that they moved into her subconscious. Dahlia's love felt more powerful and absent then; her empathy for others had returned, yet for herself it had descended to the depths of oblivion. Here, Dahlia's suicidal desires were conceived.

* * *

The recollection of her odyssey to love others again, or rather, to feel that love for others again (after all, wasn't her months-long endeavor to protect others a manifestation of love?), slowly sobered Dahlia as her current surroundings came into focus. She was leaning on the railroad crossing sign as she pretended to be engaged in her powered-off phone, her back to the tracks. Induced by the distant sound of an approaching locomotive, horror washed over her at how close she allowed herself to cease existing. However, an image of the train conductor's expression and post-trauma of failing to prevent himself from dismembering a human being unleashed a fresh surge of tumultuous, self-destructive guilt.

Dahlia strolled to the adjacent woods as the memory of getting into an argument with her mom that night overlaid the present. In those moments, she couldn't remember the fine details of the conflict's origin or content, but she knew it had been explosive despite the absence of yells; she had conditioned herself to automatically feel others' painful emotions as if they were her own, and her fear of others feeling her agony had guided her into trapping their negative emotions with hers.

Dahlia sensed that she had been persistently rude because her soul was weary, and her hatred at herself for talking down to her mom only fed the caged agony.

A memory transported Dahlia to the Beautiful Produce & More grocery store seventeen months ago.

\* \* \*

She was a stocker for the small organization (she had been fired from Hallelujah Comics because writer's block, exhaustion, and anxiety about accepting help led her to bypass deadlines). Dahlia felt herself implode during yet another day as she mechanically, yet skillfully, fulfilled her job. Her boss, Corin Durrell, was going through his ritual of verbally beating her coworker, Natalia Rathbone, for a perceived mistake. Natalia was just sixteen years old, and even quieter than Dahlia. Nary a coworker or customer stood up for her, or to him, during these attacks, even when her struggle to prevent her tears from spilling over in public was apparent. Dahlia finally overcame the debilitating shame at the irony of an unremembered event.

Corin paused while the terror and uncertainty from Natalia's expression at seeing Dahlia approach their boss with determination and a box cutter appeared to rapidly infect him. Dahlia stopped a couple of paces from her stunned boss, and she cut her forearm. "Don't ever fucking talk to her or anyone else like that again, Corin," she stated with incongruous calmness.

With fear and fury, Corin replied, "Who the fuck do you think you are, you crazy b…" He faltered when Dahlia made a cut closer to her wrist.

"This one is for calling me crazy," Dahlia added as she lowered the blade to her wrist.

"Stop it!" The power of Natalia's strength in voice and physicality, and speed, shocked Dahlia as the teenager wrenched the blade away and locked her in a hug. Dahlia felt unexpected tears pour from her as the kid wept into her shoulder. She let the blade drop as she returned her embrace. "Let's get the fuck out of here, sister," Natalia whispered between sobs.

Dahlia chuckled when she recalled that event with Natalia and their venture to Narwhal's Italian Ice soon after her arm was bandaged. She apologized again for her behavior as they ate their flavored slush and made plans for what jobs they would seek together. By the end of their third cups, their daydreams had turned wild.

They eventually lost touch as life led them down different paths, but as Dahlia viciously shivered amid the bald ebony trees, that memory unlocked other fond recollections that were abducted that night; one such remembrance involved witnessing the joy on some of her fellow college students' faces as she surreptitiously watched them read the anonymous, personal messages that she authored and stealthily left on their desks and textbooks.

Dahlia then recalled being generous with joyous laughter and an exemplar of optimism and hope as a child.

Dahlia tried to unearth the locker room memory of assault that was relayed and corroborated by others in an attempt to confront a possibility for her melancholy's rapid descent, but she accidentally found an earlier suppressed recollection; she ran from the vague event of being sexually assaulted by a distant relative before she could see it coalesce, and her focus sped toward her loving memories. The internal recreation of some of these past moments featured a third grade classmate named Brett Lenore.

* * *

Brett was Dahlia's first friend among her peers, who she felt had appreciated her, even loved her, as they would a riotous but funny animal at the zoo (like a seal), while her human mind was trapped inside one of these creatures and her attempts at communicating with them was confined to the amusing animal's abilities. Brett saw through her goofy, clumsy, silent movie-like persona and deduced that she yearned for others' attention, even as she loved brightening their moods. He sensed the loneliness within Dahlia. So Brett, popular though he was, set aside time to hang out with her and patiently waited for her. Though Dahlia still couldn't sense a connection between her soul with anyone, she was ecstatic that someone was interested in her beyond superficiality, and she couldn't believe that she was engaging in conversations beyond pleasantries; she felt as if Brett taught her to fly when she didn't even know she had wings. However, she misconstrued the small signs of melancholy within his bliss, which flitted through his eyes, as steadfast concern for her. So when Brett's illusion of bliss was misplaced one day, she was unprepared for the seemingly endless tidal wave of grief that surged from him, unspoken.

Dahlia was frightened that his silence on that day was an expression of surfaced repressions of weakening interest and increasing weariness of her. Panicked, she wondered whether Brett was only ever her friend because of pity, even as she was terrified that her agonizing loneliness, miraculously debilitated as it was, had somehow transferred to him. As they spent time at recess, she eventually, gently, told him that he should quit stressing about her and cheer up. Brett furiously responded that Dahlia wasn't the only one who struggled with depression, and though he didn't blame her for not noticing his pain since it was never his intention to reveal it to her and he felt guilt about failing to give her joy this time, he asserted that she was ignorantly selfish. Brett hesitated in his departure as Dahlia tearfully tried to articulate a lengthy apology.

Brett and Dahlia managed to become polite acquaintances afterward though even this relationship was one of impermanence. The more time they spent away from rekindling their friendship, the more difficult it became for them to resist drifting apart.

Dahlia's intertwined memory of bliss and heartache reignited her regret over frequently imposing self-isolation, nurtured by a sixth grade memory.

* * *

As soon as the bell rang, Dahlia had gone to the far end of a crowded table where she and her friends routinely congregated for lunch. They had introduced themselves and invited her into their group after they noticed her sitting alone during the first couple weeks of the school year. As she ate a PB&J sandwich, she eagerly waited for them to exit the line.

Dahlia was thrilled and anxious at the prospect of gifting her creation to Roshanda Tate during her birthday, who she considered beautiful; she had painted a five-by-eleven-inch portrait of her, Alexi Faust, Zora Vo, and herself standing before a cloudless blue sky, with goofy grins and arms around one another's shoulders. Dahlia considered the 2-D renditions of her and her friends to be mighty distant from realistic, like stick figures who wore blocky clothing and frizzy wigs, even though she spent five hours the previous night trying to perfect her painting. Still, she was quite sure that they would appreciate her heartfelt endeavor. Dahlia rarely said anything to them throughout their time together, but she intently listened as they freely conversed with one another.

Roshanda, Alexi, and Zora exited the line together with glorious smiles, but before Dahlia could excitedly wave them over, they headed for the exit without even glancing her way. Dahlia clutched her painting as an icicle pierced her heart and ceaselessly melted cold tears into her bloodstream. She feared that she was never truly close to this tight-knit trio who had known each other from elementary school; their dynamic wasn't one that she shared with them. Yet she couldn't understand why they would invite her to sit with them when they noticed her all alone and didn't at least invite her to wherever they were heading to at that moment. When she realized that they may have merely forgotten her in their excitement over celebrating Roshanda's birthday, she wept without caring about the tears that ran across her painting. Thereafter, Dahlia made a habit of avoiding the three friends and eating elsewhere on campus, where she could sit alone.

* * *

As harrowing flashbacks continued to slam into Dahlia, she attempted a new tactic to overcome her fall toward death. Within her remembrances, she sensed that suppressing painful emotions allowed them to thrive, so she allowed them to wash over her while she looked at her memories from more objective angles; through this endeavor, she realized that her self-isolation was born from a fear of rejection, and through this, she understood that she had fulfilled her own prophecy.

Dahlia received a visualization of battering her melancholy as it jeered at her, only for her misapprehension to drift away; it was a double of herself cowering before her blows. Startled, she stopped as her bloodied doppelgänger cried, "Why are you hurting me?"

It was as if the bones of Dahlia's soul bent inward as she barely progressed through a force field on her way home, while a demon in angel's clothing sang a sorrow-free version of her life into her mind's eye that would be fulfilled if she would stay. An epiphany arrived: Dahlia saw that the element of surprise was critical to her suicidal impulses, so she made an ironic vow to always remember that she was prone to receive them, without indulging their sociopathic reasoning.

As Dahlia imagined carrying her doppelgänger upon her shoulders, she silently proclaimed, "I don't want to die. Please let me survive." Her consciousness fell nearly twenty feet from a thick tree line at the edge of the woods.

# Chapter IV

## Red Fox

Eleanor Noelle remembered a night where she had an arm draped around Dahlia.

"Where does it hurt, baby girl, and what is causing this pain?" she inquired of her eight-year-old daughter, who was sniffling upon her bed. Dahlia pointed to her heart but she allowed a few moments to pass before she averted her eyes and hesitantly relayed that one of her kid cousins referred to Eleanor with a derogatory name.

Because of her parents' nurture, Eleanor had developed a keen ability to deprive dehumanizing rhetoric of its power by realizing that lies couldn't convert truths, no matter how vehemently or frequently they were uttered; in this way, she embraced her value as a fellow soul of humanity. However, panic and rage entered the outskirts of Eleanor's feelings as she wondered how a child discovered that word, about her daughter finding out about it too, and how in the world she would navigate to a response that was suitable for her young daughter.

"I don't care what anyone says. You're beautiful and my mommy," Dahlia responded.

Eleanor embraced her daughter, and as she wept, she realized that a fear of being rejected by her daughter had entered the outskirts of her awareness.

After Dahlia asked her mom if she would be okay, Eleanor assured her, "Sometimes people cry when they feel happy."

Eleanor's mind wandered ahead to her argument with Dahlia, some hours before she rose from her bed to get a drink of water, and found her daughter's note on the kitchen table.

The memory of her daughter subtly mocking Christianity that night was due to bottled anger and that morning's transphobic sermon whose facade was love. Dahlia reluctantly apologized for thrashing the faith, before she blurted to her mom, "Why did you tell the pastor about your identity? You should have known how it would turn out. Christians will never accept you, especially a transgender woman who they inherently deem a man who made himself neither male or female, or who they look at with closeted lust."

Eleanor knew that Dahlia didn't mean for her last statement to be an insult and that she was reacting out of fear for her, but she still made her irritation known about Dahlia dismissing every Christian, including herself and Karlo. She also expressed disappointed hurt, though it came out as rage, that her daughter continued to implicitly reveal that she no longer considered herself a believer.

Eleanor inwardly cursed Karlo for locking himself in his home studio with his latest illustration project for Ebony Lion Comics, a rival to Hallelujah Comics; though she knew this latest project was especially heartfelt, since he had dedicated this latest venture to them as a family, and she loved him for it, she wished he was in this room, lending her his support.

Eleanor closed the argument by conveying, "The things which are purest are ripe to be twisted by some people to cause the most harm. Do not confuse God with the hurt souls who claim to be his followers while dehumanizing others; truths do not become lies, no matter how often or forcefully liars say otherwise.

"Also, I remind you that you are my daughter. You will not talk down to me again."

* * *

Eleanor's attention was captured by a spot of red slowly moving upon an ivory floor and between ebony trunks. She and Karlo felt like they lost what little sanity that remained as they instinctively left their car in front of the tracks and followed the red fox at the edge of the adjacent woods; some other members of the small search team quickly pursued. The fox ran deeper into the forest, and it seemed to follow faint footprints that became apparent to the parents as they got closer. As her husband loudly expressed that he found something substantive, Eleanor remembered meeting him and his daughter for the first time, in-person.

* * *

Karlo had agreed to join her community-sponsored poetry slam with his daughter; after the event, they ate mustard-smothered veggie dogs, air-fried onion rings, and honeyed Italian ices at Narwhal's. As they conversed, Eleanor's infatuation with Karlo developed into a familial love for him and his daughter. When Karlo left to order one more round of ices (ones sweetened with brown sugar this time), a five year old Dahlia looked up at Eleanor with wide, gleaming eyes and loudly asked with the most joyous smile, "Are you going to be my mom?"

* * *

Eleanor's legs gave way when she saw Dahlia on the snow, though Karlo and the paramedics continued to run to her. Karlo's memory of his daughter taking her first steps toward him at home played as if it were happening now, even as he saw himself close the distance between himself and Dahlia in the woods. He silently promised that he would spend more time with his family as a memory resurfaced from his young adulthood of his father banging and breaking open a bathroom door to find his younger brother dead from a self-inflicted wound.

Karlo tearfully prayed that Dahlia would be okay as he cradled her. Eleanor broke into sobs when the paramedic confirmed that she was alive, breathing well, and responding.

Dahlia lived.

# Book II

# Dahlia Noelle's Literary Art

## The Super Short Fiction

# Chapter I

## Humor Numbs My Pain, While Tragic Art Heals Me

### Beautiful, Bizarre, and Tragic

Friendship is peculiar and beautiful. It is individuals treating each other as family. It's enjoying one another's presence as laughter erodes the floodgates to tears, and as embraces heat souls that are frostbitten by fear.

Yet no person prepares us for the camaraderie that blooms through our souls wilting while life leads most of us upon different paths. Still, we have some knowledge of its expiration, whispered by premonition, when we desperately try to immerse ourselves in those shared beautiful moments: as we attempt to send time in a loop around us amid unspoken gratefulness, abstract aches, the last encounter's stealthy arrival, and familial love.

### Stars and Electricity

Anxiety transforms a nervous system into a tangle of uninsulated electrical wires, and melancholy is a neutron star of loneliness.

### Break-In

The Grim Reaper's strange sons bang on my doors and windows,
as some drag their talons through my attic's floorboards, that hive
of creatures named Suicide.

### Hush

Hush, little baby, don't make others cry,
all your troubles will soon away fly.
Now rest your weary head, my child,
for peace with you will reconcile.
Before you repair Sorrow's smiling mask,
the choo-choo train will accomplish her task.
As your head transforms and gets carried away,
nary a soul will hang their head in dismay.
For the moment I carry thee,
will be the breath that sets them free.
Hush, little baby, we don't wish harm on anyone,
we want your burden to fly away from everyone.
Twenty-three years, you've been here too long.
Now we are going to right this wrong.

# Chapter II

## My Humor Unleashes Laughter in the Crowd, and I'm the Only One Laughing

### Legacy

C.A. Nicholas frees a sigh which flies forth and dejectedly sinks through the surrounding air.

C.A. NICHOLAS:

"Well, gosh…fuckin' darn. Maybe I'll finally
be famous after I die."

Three weeks later, Nicholas's heart surprised everyone, especially its young host, by embarking on an early retirement. What a bloody fucker.

Nicholas gets buried alongside some of the Greats. Every person who stands before his grave ruminates, "Who the hell is this dipshit?"

Meanwhile, at Heaven's Gates, Nicholas runs toward God, exhilaration coursing through his gait and joy shining through his tear-stained face. God smiles as He opens His arms in invitation.

As Nicholas approaches Him, he realizes that the Divine Being was warmly gesturing at a ladybug that had stealthily landed between his eyes.

As the teeny-weeny creature flies from Nicholas's forehead to join the humans and other beings in Heaven, God turns to the unwitting ladybug taxi. The Divine Being grins, places a hand on Nicholas's shoulder.

GOD:
"Who are you?"

### Dear Pastor Abigail

Dear Pastor Abigail,

The God in *Legacy* isn't a true representation of God! I still believe in Him! I meant no offense by my story or my character named C.A. Nicholas!

You agreed with me on humor's power to bring relief during bad days, and even transform them into good ones, with the right perspective; please don't hate me.

By the way, I forgot that there was a saucy book in the Bible; other than King Solomon comparing his lover's teeth with sheep (better than relating them to coal), her hair with goats (what?), and her eyes with doves (did they fly away?), the *Song of Songs* rules. I'm being serious here. It's so erotic, I love it!

# 666

Dear Dahlia,

No worries! You didn't have to explain yourself; part of what made your story amusing is the incongruity of reality with your fiction.

Also, the *Song of Songs*, while no less important than the other parts of the Bible, isn't written in a style to my liking. However, I love *Proverbs* and *Ecclesiastes*.

By the way, some of our fellow Christians are so terrified of the number 666. I'm curious about how many of our fellow siblings in humanity have the patience to count the stars (I certainly lack patience) and what happens when they arrive at the 666th one. Do they blow raspberries at that poor gassy creation, even if it is still alive?

If any are census takers, then what happens if they arrive at the 666th human being? Do they whip out holy water from a side holster and suddenly spray it onto the unsuspecting soul?

And what happens if they have a Bible with at least 666 pages? Do our spiritual family members frantically rip out that page or quickly slam the scriptures shut, avert their eyes, and give a nervous whistle?

Love,
Pastor Abigail

P.S. It's so nice to have someone to talk to. I was grateful enough that you created me!

## Believers' Rage

Do you ever wonder why some people feel fury toward the individuals who tell them that God doesn't exist?

Well, it's because they know that the news may reach God's ears, and if it does He'll mutter, "How embarrassing! I wish someone told me sooner," as He dissipates Himself.

Do you also wonder why some Atheists experience rage toward those who tell them that God is real?

Well, they know that God will exist if people believe hard enough. They realize that He'll then peer through the doors of each of their agnostic closets and they'll have to eventually acknowledge that there's no one else in there whom He's giving a cheery wave to.

## Goodbye, My Hero

Joby hugs himself tight as a cyclone of agony sends a surge of tears through his levee of composure. He is attending Goby's funeral.

As a sequence of sobs detonates throughout his unsheltered soul, he again whispers to himself, "He sacrificed his life for mine."

A sad, honest clown named Foby walks up to the podium and commences with his eulogy for Goby; Goby, who jumped in front of a blade that was meant for Joby.

Joby strives to rebuild his facade of calm as Foby's speech continues to unfurl, but he loses his composure when the eulogizer utters with a great sigh:

"Bless Goby. Not many knew that he had an unbidden desire to die and…"

"What the fuck!?" Joby yells amid a sob.

### The Choo-Choo and I

I am C.A. Nicholas, a human with a head of lettuce.

Amid a downpour, and full of despair, I kneel near an automaton butcher at the top of a hill. I longingly look at his blade as I rub my neck.

C.A. NICHOLAS:

"Will I ever be worthy enough to belong with the most beloved, among they who include me as the most loved?

"Yet who would I be if I had achieved everything, and there was nothing else to dream?"

I stand up quickly and slip. My neck lands upon a potato with many blinking eyes, inches from the butcher's incoming blade. My head rolls down the rocky slope, toward the town, and it sings the following in the stylings of a dirge, yet with a fast tempo.

C.A. NICHOLAS:

"Oh, what have I done? But hallelujah, I am not done! However, my head is on the run. At least I can still sing this run. Yet this sensation isn't so very fun. And…OOOUCH, son of a gun!"

The automaton sings the following with a falsetto voice, in the style of an opera, as he looks at my headless self.

AUTOMATON:

"Icky! Iiiiiicky, iiiiiiiiicky! ICKYYYYYY!"

A hermit on the hill emerges from a cave and tenderly takes my hands in his claws as a gleeful tune plays; he dances side-to-side with me. But I am tragically quite clumsy since I'm unable to see where I'm going, which is making him a bit irritated. Still, I don't want to dance. I want my head back!

Unfortunately, a headless chicken places my head on his neck, and he ecstatically flies away.

## A Ghost and a Blustery November

DAHLIA:

"I'm off to see the neighbor, my wonderful neighbor across the way."

Dahlia, clad in an emo outfit, daintily skips out of her ground floor apartment and across the busy street with a gift balanced upon her left palm. She expertly swerves around speeding cars as drivers honk and wave their greetings; all roll down their windows and bid Dahlia a good afternoon while some even high-five her…all without slowing down of course, before other passersby effortlessly jump out of their vehicles and break into a musical number with her.

When the song and dance routine ends, Dahlia continues to the apartment complex across the street. She turns around and sees a grown White man, covered with a white sheet (there are no eye holes in the sheet, but there are ear holes of course) at the end of her apartment, and he beckons her over.

Fortunately, the sheet doesn't have a pointed hood. Unfortunately for the belated trick-or-treater, Dahlia would like to be on her way just the same. So she points to her package and shouts, with a smile,

DAHLIA:

"I'm on a special errand, and I've already allowed too much time to flee from me!"

So Dahlia carries on, right up to the front door of her neighbor, which is on the top floor. She huffs, and she puffs, and she doesn't blow the neighbor's home down. She's merely attempting to catch her breath. When she's breathing like a gentlewoman again, she smooths her naturally black ponytail (which she's dyed ebony) and politely hammers on the door.

As Dahlia waits for a response, she peeks around the corner of her apartment complex and her heart calmly convulses as the Ghost Man is still standing there…watching her…waiting for her to finish…sharpening his butter knife…humming Barney's theme song with impossible loudness. (Wait, no; thank goodness that lullaby is coming from a Parrot walking out of an alley.)

NEIGHBOR:

"Hey Dahlia…thank you so much for delivering this! Will you please thank your mom for making yet another make-believe cake for me?"

Dahlia glances at the fake ghost and sees him preoccupied with slicing a bagel who is fighting to remain whole.

BAGEL:

"Eat me as I am!"

NEIGHBOR:

"Hey Dahlia, is everything okay?"

Dahlia grins as she says,

DAHLIA:

"Not at all! Have a beautiful day!"

Dahlia thrusts the dessert of love and air into her neighbor's hands as she runs through the apartment, through the open rear window, and down the fire escape to the rear of the building. She's about to make her way around, but she suddenly realizes what a pickle she is still in.

DAHLIA:

"The Ghost Man is bound to have won his bagel battle by now, so he must be keeping a keen eye out, wondering where I've gone and impatiently waiting for my return. How awkward will it be when he plainly sees me walking back to my apartment, but from the opposite side of this building? What will I say? 'No, Mr. Ghost Man, I wasn't avoiding you...I was avoiding you with force.'

"Yeah, real swell, Dahlia.

"I think I'll walk out of this city, around it, and through it from the other side so I can end up in the alleyway behind my building, without being seen. I'll climb the fire escape and break through my home's rear window. Oh, what a relief!"

BOY KID WHO HAD BEEN
LISTENING TO DAHLIA'S SPEECH
SINCE A MONOLOGUE WOULD BE
POINTLESS WITHOUT AN
AUDIENCE (BOY KID):
"Epilogue…your sad self sits in the rear of a police car because the neighbors called the cops about a burglary."

DAHLIA:
"What?"

BOY KID:
"Breaking into your apartment sure wouldn't look suspicious. Anyways, who's to say that you won't proceed to rob your own home? You're crazy enough, with your monologuing and all."

Dahlia mumbles to herself as she distractedly turns the corner of her friend's apartment complex and walks toward her home. Ghost Man confusedly scratches his head as Dahlia comes into view from the far side of the building.

Boy Kid walks alongside Dahlia; she is still too far away to be heard by Ghost Man. Boy Kid hopes that Dahlia's next monologue is brief so that he can get on with his life already.

### DAHLIA:

"I'm not afraid of him, you know. It's just that I'm uncomfortable with conversations…"

### BOY KID:

"You don't say."

### DAHLIA:

"I didn't finish talking."

### BOY KID:

"You did, but you decided to make an unnecessary sequel. Please have mercy on my life and your ears; do stop talking."

Dahlia stops walking in the middle of the road.

BOY KID:

"Have mercy on my soul!"

Meanwhile, EMTs, police officers, and others don't complain as they smoothly drive their vehicles around the two individuals.

DAHLIA:

"I was going to say that I'm uncomfortable with having conversations with him. He's not a bad individual…he's like Casper…friendly and all; he's harmless. It's just that he often asks for me to tell him a story, of which he has an addiction to; my imagination is experiencing a drought."

BOY KID:

"At least it's not a drinking problem like what I have. Ah, no matter how hard I try, my poor soul can't bring the bottle to my lips!"

DAHLIA:

"Don't you know that I'm not in the mood to laugh right now?"

BOY KID:

"Yes, I do. Did you have to write me so sarcastically!? My name is Damien Noelle, not 'Boy Kid.'"

Dahlia and Damien resume walking.

DAHLIA:

"Also, on the first day we crossed paths, he…"

DAMIEN:

"I'm getting tired of this movie. Ah, finally, Ghost Man is within earshot. Goodbye!"

Damien teleports himself way out of there.

Dahlia and Ghost Man embarrassingly stare at one another; they are inches away. Well, she thinks Ghost Man is, but she can't see his eyes clearly. Dahlia tentatively waves and Ghost Man does the same. She slumps her head, enters her home, and quickly shuts the door.

### Dahlia's Drug

Little did Dahlia know, when her five-year-old self slapped a "count on me to be drug free" sticker on her bedroom window, that she'd grow up to be a coffee drinkin' enthusiast. Nor did she expect her sticker to gain sentience.

The following scene takes place in Dahlia's bedroom, close to midnight.

STICKER:

"Yer a junkie, mwe-he-he-he!!!"

DAHLIA:

"What the…!?"

STICKER:

"Ya child self would be disgusted if she could see ya self now. Me? I'm tickled by the irony and ya couldn't scrub me off this glass pane even if ya gave enough of a care to. Ya naive like Peter Prickin' Pan; ya've joined the horde in gettin' off ta one of the most socially accepted drugs."

DAHLIA:

"Since when did you talk, and what are you talking about?"

Dahlia sips from two coffee mugs simultaneously.

DAHLIA:

"Well, I confess that I am chained to a popular compulsion. I get so jittery when I don't give in, you see. I must allow my groping fingers to unearth treasure from the twin caves that keep on giving."

STICKER:

"What?"

DAHLIA:

"You know…picking my…"

Dahlia puts a finger in each nostril.

STICKER:

"Stop it! I'm talkin' 'bout ya coffee lovin.' Ya and ya ilk should wisen up enough to begin a Coffee Addicts Anonymous program. Oooh! Ya club should be called C.A.A.N., for Coffee Addicts Anonymous Nincompoops!

"Mwe-he-he…oh!"

Dahlia had set her drinks down as she reached for Sticker.

Dahlia rips him off with a solitary swipe, and repeatedly dunks and swirls him in the mugs of coffee in rapid succession.

DAHLIA:

"Who's the addict now!?"

STICKER:

"Will…"

*Splash!*

STICKER:

"…ya…"

*Splash!*

STICKER:

"…calm…"

*Splash!*

STICKER:

"…ma…"

*Splash!*

STICKER:

"…dance!"

*Splash!*

Dahlia approaches her senses as she stops her dunking and stirring frenzy. She realizes that most of the coffee has leapt out of the mugs and she begins to sob. Sticker believes that Dahlia is crying for him, yet he cares not. After all, he has no lungs to drown (but how does he speak?!) or nerves to scorch. Nor does he worry over Dahlia's knowledge of these things; she would never react as an entitled child who was scorned if it led to the murder or injury of poor Mister Sticker. All the sticky (and currently drenched) paper lad cares about is a proper drink!

Sticker dives from Dahlia's loosening grasp to slurp the dregs of coffee in the nearest mug.

\* \* \*

Later that night, Dahlia authentically apologizes as she and Sticker sit upon the roof, meditate upon the stars, and share a fresh pot of coffee. A prolonged gust of wind carries Sticker away, but unfortunately Dahlia doesn't notice since she's engrossed in one of her monologues. Nor does Sticker cry out since he remembered that he doesn't have lungs to speak. After Dahlia finishes her speech to an audience of one, she looks at the place where Sticker sat.

DAHLIA:

"…Oh."

Dahlia jumps up and looks around. But Sticker is long gone.

## You Play That Starfish, Oh So Wonderfully!

Many men believe that women can experience pleasance if they merely perform a two-step rhythm within the sweltering and snug southern embraces, with their hanging inflatables. They too believe in miracles since they're of the notion that women can rocket to euphoria when they catapult molten ivory beyond their lovers' lower lips.

Oh, don't even get me started on the art[lessness] of playing a starfish. Dear fellow men who're attracted to women, why wouldn't you want to thoroughly love your soul mates instead of treating them as autonomous pleasure toys?

By the way, I'm so sorry if I've offended you. My greatest desire is to gain your approval (obviously).

## An Ode for Outcasts

Spoken Intro

Are there any who hate the ones who tag-along?
Is your peace blighted by they who are too-tight thongs?

Verse 1

Oh, there's a circus for every one of you,

and there is no fee, so enter if you please!

Lookie, lookie, just behind,

a tent of red you will find.

Its name must be pleasant to you lovely curs,

*The Logical Love to Loath these Amateurs*!

## Chorus

Oh, truly, it's logical to hate the ones with insecure hearts,

natural to be displeased by those embodiments of haunting farts.

I know you're immersed in woe, but I see your smiles, and that's
a start.

You must be exhausted by they who should be excommunicated
from the smart.

Though intelligence from your excellent antithesis of excellence
departs,

May your spirits be lifted by relating to our woefully-created tarts!

## Verse 2

My, oh my, cast your sight far to the right,

there's a tent that'll give you quite the fright!

Why, it's an edifice of dour yellow,

accompanied by lights of vile neon green.

Perfectly reflected, you shall be seen, and its title will warm your
spleen,

*The Supremely Obtuse and Phenomenally Projecting Human Beings*!

Verse 3

Shift your vision to the left and perceive a tent of invisible gray.

If the other attractions failed to thrill you, this one will improve your day!

Its salty appellation shall captivate you,

You'll finally be awarded all that you're due.

Its name shall tickle your fancies into tears since you are flawless imperfections,

*Their Intelligence in Emotionality Exists in Imaginations.*

# Chapter III

## I Continue to Cry After My Laughter Dies

### Belonging

Her soul tries again to break through friendship's force field, from acquaintanceship's domain, yet "How can I," she thinks, "when I can't even master the dance of fluent conversation?

"I try and I strive to speak their language, which interlaces souls with one another, yet I remain an island among them, an adrift cosmonaut, untethered from humanity's intimate symphonic choir. How do I articulate in a way that invites not merely sympathy (even when my speech isn't late on arrival, a sputtering staccato, or someone who has abandoned me), but love?

"Yet isn't sympathy a manifestation of love? Is it selfish for me to desire more than their knowledge of my existence and generous kindness to someone whose existence is crippled? Don't I perceive them striving to find me, someone who's nearly invisible, endeavoring to befriend an enigma? Do I mistake acquaintanceship for their friendship? Aren't there many forms of dancing with camaraderie? Do I conflate some of its styles as only true, or as more loving than the dance which we share, as if love is capable of having lesser forms?"

Still, she now ponders upon how much of herself she has altered. She knows the yearning to belong is universal, and upon this contemplation, she realizes that many whom she loves may also be expert thespians who wear masks which contradict their souls drowning in melancholia.

After a wealth of introspection, she realizes that, "Humanity's universal desperation to belong is why so many of us kill certain aspects of our identities. Even so, some of us go beyond chipping away portions of our souls by ripping out what remains to replace them with corporately synthesized ones; while those echoes of love are still not guaranteed from they who are blind to others' inherent magnificence.

"Likewise," she intones, "I already recognize that people's dehumanizing statements about me don't magic falsehoods into truth, yet I must also relay that acceptance which is gained after striving for it is that which is easily lost; that form of belonging is as stable as a house of cards, absent of roots and tenuous to circumstances' tremors."

Behold, Authentic Acceptance's creed: "There is nothing more that you can do to make me love you more. You are wonderful as you are."

## Nine Doors

Anxiety is finding myself in a room with nine doors that lead to horror. One door leads to freedom. All the doors are unmarked.

Depression is every dream taunting me, a Hall of Fame for my failures which I perceive, and a window to paradise from the prison cell of hell.

## I'm Hurting Too

We're not failures to they who genuinely love. Nor are we frail or life's abomination. Relief won't embrace us if we slam our skulls until exhaustion implores us to cease, or if our nose pours scarlet estuaries. Nor will it end if we bludgeon inky lagoons into existence beneath our skin, or unearth crimson oil from our wrists. Nor will we free ourselves, nor the rest of they who love us, by self-annihilation. These are the truths which we must forever remember.

## Who Are They Who Judge Melancholic Souls?

The souls who judge they who have melancholia choose to deflect attention from their own insecurities. They do so whether ignorance clouds their minds, guilt of the same affliction drowns their selfless proclivities, or denial distracts their fear of being uprooted from the self-perceived shallow soil of their bliss.

## An Invisible and Predatory Portal Within Melancholia

May you never be abducted by, or may you never again be set adrift within, that haunting dimension in Melancholia. There lies the dimension where personal hopes go to die upon losing faith in their existence, and Time causes lost wanderers to move in slow motion while Society speeds on by, and Time, alongside Gravity, forces preyed upon souls to unceasingly implode.

In that domain, unrelenting Nostalgia (intertwined with visions of fantasized Joy) mocks prisoners while the portal to living within them is sealed. And in that place, there are disoriented souls whose spiritual tethers to others don't merely feel disconnected, but annihilated, immune to socialization.

May the currency of grace free beyond some whom Circumstance seemingly sentenced to live there for life, and not cease until every debt is satisfied.

## Expressing Melancholy is Beautiful

There is beauty in expressing happiness when it is there, though too often much of society deems any emotion that doesn't at least imitate frequent joy as an affront to morality. Yet the exasperation from they who indulge in implicit condemnation is sorrowful; it may arise from a fear, borne upon memories, that the bliss which they fantasized into believing is eternal can't possibly be so.

## Healer of Souls

I'm a healer of souls, though I've discovered that I'm a contagious pathogen whose uplifting presence is a precursor to plummets into despondency. I learned that I'm ultimately a destroyer, enslaved by destiny, who makes the disease of hopelessness its most effective by leading people into emotional triumph, only to have that manifestation of paradise snatched away as their souls are torn apart by raging melancholy.

So I paid Isolation to annihilate the ties between myself and my loved ones as I prayed that their souls could still be saved from me. Too weak, I rebuilt transient connections because my perpetually lonely soul yearns for any semblance of belonging; though deep down in my heart, I know that I'm an anomaly who could never be fully loved by they whose blood doesn't course through me; hot scarlet estuaries which flow from my unearthed veins and upon my arms to my bedroom's paneled floor. As exhaustion compels me to kneel, I sense an individual of ivory light catch me before my head slams upon the ground.

"Dear child, why do you exhaust yourself?" the luminous being inquires in a voice like a choir as he strokes my hair in the golden rays of the setting sun. I raised a slit forearm to point at the center of my chest where a cavernous hole festers, an old cavity that is invisible to passersby. The being holds me closer to his warm bosom as he caresses me, and he asks the next rhetorical question: "Do you love them?"

"I love them," I proclaim through a fresh deluge of tears as I see each one of my loved ones and whisper their names.

"Then arise. You know what you must do to set them and yourself free!" the creature sings as he places the sharpened knife within my palm. "I won't leave you," the Grim Reaper and Melancholy's son tenderly whispers as a lullaby flows past his lips.

Violently trembling, I set my tainted blade's edge upon a vein within my neck with his help.

I don't want to die (but I don't want to live in unceasing agony). I don't desire for anyone to cry from my demise (but I will ultimately set them free from myself). Yes, I will bring them liberation (no, they love me).

I hear the cadences of their laughter, the rhythms of their speech, and the tones of all of their voices (I am a part of their beautiful experiences), and I see the joy reflected upon the outward aspects of the artistry whom they are as they socialize with one another (I am thoroughly loved too).

Oh, but imagine the eventual bliss when I'm no longer there to fail them (I am not a god). I am only human (they have their struggles and they will never be burdens.) I will never be a failure (nor will they). I will always be loved (as I will forever love them).

Wait! I am not a pathogen. Truth is not swayed by falsehoods.

I shriek at the monstrosity in angel's guise, forcing that master manipulator to flee by my resolve as the embers of sunlight vanish. Flashes of my loved ones having my soul ripped from theirs manifests before me as I perceive what it would feel like to have their souls torn from mine through suicide. I force the images of their collapsing bodies, afflicted by new widening craters in their chests, and the sound of their reverberating wails to give way to our beautiful memories and shared futures; embracing one another's souls through woes and triumphs.

There is no such thing as a perfect day, but every day is perfectly worth living.

## What Is True Beauty?

Many kind hearts lead countless souls into the assurance that beauty is solely exempt from appearance. Such comforting gestures may be enfolded in such wrappings as "true beauty comes from within" or "I didn't marry you for your looks." They are ever delivered with the almighty backhanded slap.

No, beauty is not solely about personality, nor the extension of it through loving behavior, but appearance as well. To deny a person's features as vacant of beauty, despite proclaiming the beauty of who shines from within, is to utter a malnourished truth, just as declaring "it's what's on the outside that matters," as impotent in kindness as assuring one "I love you because you look hot."

The fault is not upon the person who is judged as being insufficient in visual merit but by the one who deemed them so.

We need to recognize our own shortcomings on assessing beauty, including cultures' major influence upon our conceptions.

## We Are Beautiful

We are perfect in our appearance.

Beauty is not lesser for bosoms of non-symmetry and level essence. Perfection doesn't abandon those whose skin displays stretched lines of victory, nor does attractiveness discriminate against anyone for keeping their inverted triangles of hair free from wax, laser, and razor.

Splendor is equal for all body types, from those with slender builds, to those who have round physiques. All hues of melanin shine with identical magnificence: ivory, ebony, and all the colors in between.

We are perfect in our appearance, but our beauty is also within.

## We Are Worthy

May we endeavor on even when we cannot perceive a light at the end of the tunnel nor perceive a sign that the void will end. Let's ever strive when agony flows within our veins via every heartbeat; we shall carry on not ultimately for the sake of potential relief, but for the benefit of those who love us, including those whom we have yet to meet. May the words of my father (Karlo Noelle) give you courage, "Worthiness arrives not from victories nor from others' praise. It is free from Acceptance's decrees. You exist; therefore, you are wonderful."

## Loved Ones, Hold On

I yearn for us to keep on loving one another holistically. Let's continue loving the cadences of one another's laughter, the rhythms of each other's conversations, and the tones of all our voices, as well as the outward aspects of the artistry of who we are. May we continue making sure that each one of our souls is heard as we champion each other's passions, while holding one another in embraces whenever agony produces tears from pierced hearts (and carry onward in embracing each other in the blissful times as well; I also pray for us to feel our heartbeat alongside another's as the warmth of our souls washes over us both).

We would do well to unceasingly fight for one another with an absence of compromise for ourselves, as well as others. Though we may guide each other whenever a path leads one of us astray, let's refuse to overburden ourselves, lest we become a victim as well, and may we take time for ourselves to properly rehabilitate our minds, spirits, and bodies. To carry onward in loving each other's existences and one another's souls is our treasure, but striving to do the same for ourselves with the same fierceness is another that is yet to be pursued.

# Book III

# Moondrop!

A Surreal Comedy by Dahlia Noelle

# Chapter I

## Not the Clouds!

Bob Tom had always wondered what it would be like to touch the clouds. However, his passion had plummeted from its peak ever since his dad told him that the exhibition of cartoons landing upon them, as if they were a giant's misplaced gravity-defying, wind-sailing cotton fluffs, was a deception. His disappointment that launched then accelerated through the stratosphere when his father told him that the clouds didn't taste like marshmallows either. Bob was forty five years old when he discovered this reality (his misperceptions had merely been caused by a smidgen of a sheltered life), and his Poppa hated to be an unmasker of these unfortunate truths, like a parent who revealed that Santa Clause didn't exist, but his son had insisted that he was going to skydive without a parachute; nevertheless, Poppa didn't have the heart to deny him Santa Clause's existence.

Bob's pappy wiped a tear away as he fondly recalled taking his son to tell a new mall Santa what he wanted this Christmas; it had transpired a few seconds ago. The senior actor in a beard (it appeared like a cotton swab quilt that was large enough to be a bedspread for Thumbelina) and scarlet outfit swore that impotency finally found him as Bob plummeted his rear end upon his lap; poor St. Nick had stretched his legs apart to get the blood flowing more freely, and he was startled by the speed and seriousness of the towering, bulging muscle man. He was subsequently shocked into just nodding along to Bob's requests as Bob interpreted the mall Santa's tears as ones of endearment.

Anyway, I shall exit that tangent and return to the main point, which is about Bob and clouds; after I tell you that when he stumbled upon the truth about Santa later that day, he stormed out of the house to become an army general.

\* \* \*

Clouds stroked Bob's aftershave-dabbed and perpetually hairless face as they flew by. The aroma reminded him of yellowing mass-market paperbacks, luxury car seats, and cigarettes. He flicked his tongue around the first puff of exhaust from his next-seat colleague's spicy cigar smoke. Bob didn't enjoy smoking, but he had been defeated by an impulse to experience even a semblance of the white fluff in the sky again. He was very recently deemed ineligible to fly on account of his heart; that and his first time on a plane was on a commercial airliner during his escape from home. He had opened the emergency hatch on their ascent to caress and taste the clouds. Somehow, Bob became a four-star general five years later, causing reality to cower before him.

Bob gazed at the luscious rainbow-colored hair, ivory-rim-bespectacled, and ebony camo-wearing woman who was projected on a towering screen at the far end of the underground war room. "Space CIA Director Mack Byron, what's the status update from that agent who's code-named Uranus?" Bob pronounced Uranus in a way that he saw as honoring tradition, that pronunciation being "your anus."

A cough slipped through Major Mads Napoleon's suppression. He was persistently the most serious looking individual that anyone in that conversation had met, and he was known to make the bladders of military boot camp instructors cry a little from fear. So when Major Napoleon made that noise like backfire, the others looked at him immediately with expectation, as if he had intended to lasso their attentions. He waved at them to resume.

"Our inside agent confirmed that the Moon is committed to invading the Earth in…approximately an hour, despite claims to the contrary," Director Byron stated. "We can still triumph, and easily sir, but Uranus is quite worried. He means no offense."

Bob replied, "None taken.

"You may tell Uranus that though he feels that the challenge appears hairy…"

Another cough cannon-balled from Mads, and he suppressed the echoes of its thunder by placing a skull-bejeweled hand to his mouth while he repeatedly slammed a fist upon the ebony marble table as if he were a judge who had misplaced his gavel in an unruly court. He wiped his gunmetal eyes with a handkerchief, which was emblazoned with burning skeletons giddily breaking through their graves and crying when they inadvertently set a town to flames. Once he regained his composure, he motioned for them to continue.

Bob remade his reply. "We will resume as planned. I know Uranus is concerned about a close shave, but…"

Mads continued to lose the battle of restraint. Laughter sporadically whistled from him, tears cascaded down his reddened cheeks, and he slapped the table with gleeful abandon.

Blame it on nerves, courage, or a delusion of immortality, but whatever Bob's inspiration in that moment was, he found himself glaring at the Major for his interruption. "Major Napoleon, have you suddenly found the prospect of Armageddon to be hilarious, or are you just amused by Uranus?"

The major's years of bottled-up laughter erupted from him as he rocketed to the ceiling and bounced around the room like a popped cork. Nearly everyone else in the room dove under the table, while Director Byron ducked under a desk behind her. Yet Bob, General Tom himself, valiantly stood and caught the Major when he entered arm's reach. "Four-Star General Lexi Dexi, open the hatch," he proclaimed to the only other person who hadn't cowered there (as his muscles and veins bulged from keeping the Major in place). "My courage is as mighty as yours!"

The red-haired, violet-eyed, freckle-chinned, and wonderfully curvy Four-Star General pounded the keypad near the war room's stairwell (at the opposite end of the projection screen). Bob released Mads under the bunker complex's open hatch, three miles above, and the Major rocketed toward that planet with a cheeky name. Bob's coworkers rapturously applauded him.

"While a dramatic entrance to save humanity brings relief to many hearts, who will be left to cheer if I keep waiting?" Bob asked the awe-struck room with tears in his eyes. He bid adieu and climbed to the Earth's surface with phenomenal speed.

# Chapter II

## Moon vs. Man!

The downtown metropolis appeared like a city set that a kid had semi-destroyed with a white, pockmarked, and circular block of cheese that had action figure limbs, while strategically placed candles mimicked burning entities.

The Moon had gracefully landed in the metropolis, and he proceeded to sprint through the area as the military's and police force's bullets stuck to him like modern art piercings, while their small explosives were no more effective than water balloons. Everyone looked hopeless in the hub of Skyscraper City. This was exemplified by a young office worker weeping as she held her coworker and lover's hand, which extended from a fallen skyscraper.

Bob decided that the time for crossing the line from observation to action had arrived, so he emerged from the shadows and placed a comforting hand on the woman's shoulder. She looked up and exclaimed, "General Bob Tom!" The reporters at hand picked up on this revelation, and the news rapidly spread from civilian bystanders in the vicinity to the news reporters on the other side of the world. Within seconds, everyone outside of the disaster zone with access to a breaking news broadcast, from a cinema house to a portable radio, who hadn't tuned in did so then. The Moon stopped splashing in the congested Pollu Pollu River, and  he swung around with circular eyes so widened that they looked as if they were captives straining against their restraints, and his mouth so quickly snapped open in shock that it appeared as if a black hole had spontaneously been born on his face.

Bob threw his space military uniform off to reveal a baby-oiled, dark brown, and freshly waxed body. The man of India's abs had compelled eight-packs everywhere into insecurity, his arms had made all bodybuilders bashful, and his legs had caused ancient sequoias to finally admire a human. Meanwhile, Bob's nipples were clothed in hot-pink pasties.

The Moon's blush spread like a time-lapsed wildfire, and it became so bright that Rudolph wept while he threw his red nose away. Simultaneously, possums passed out with the largest grins, and a distracted rookie reporter accidentally allowed a camera to linger on a human mother breast-feeding her baby boy ("What's bloody wrong with you?" a senior reporter shouted as he beat the young man up. "Don't you know the kiddies are watching? If you can't get a shot of General Bob or the Moon, then keep filming the massacre!")

The Riders of Infinity band picked their bloodless jaws off the floor, crunched them back into place, and rocked the

General's theme song at a nearby amphitheater. The lead singer of the zombies, Ben Benny Bernard, belted:

"General Bob Tom conquered that Martian named Santa,
'He's undefeatable,' that's humanity's mantra!
World hunger starved to death,
Thank the General for that and for saving my daughter Beth!
Our leader made sure we no longer need to pee or poo,
So to extinction, each of us can scream, 'Have a loo,
yeah!'
To fight our hero is to succeed in failure,
I swear I'm not a soothsayer!
It's just as immutable as the Law of Gravity,
To contradict this truth is to be one with vanity!
General Bob Tom, General Bob Tom, General Bob Tom!"

General Bob, with his six-foot-seven tall and skin-toned, nylon-briefs wearing self, charged at the 400-foot-high space rock. As he swiftly depleted the mile between his enemy in the Moon's blush-ignited night, he proclaimed, "Only the stupid fight me!"

Bob soared through the scarlet-colored sky for a couple of blocks before he crashed through the TALLEST TOWER EVAHs penthouse. The Moon had lightly back slapped him.

Anyway, Bob soared on as he collided into an innocent bystander, and they crashed through the opposite window. They fell to the street below. That's how Bob's life ended. Let the end credits roll and try to enjoy the music. Sorry, not every story is meant to have a Happily Ever After. There's really no need to be sad, stop it, you're going to make me cry, and oh, fine! I'm joking! Bob didn't die! He's alive, oh may joy continue to thrive, he's alive!

Even though Bob fell from the 213th story, he had landed on the bystander, so of course he was alive. He grumbled "Ouch" before he hauled himself up and firmly shook the hand of the unfortunate man. "Thank you, bystander."

"Kick the Moon's ass for me, won't you General Bob Tom?" the bystander whispered before his life departed.

The bystander wasn't bloody, but he was as flattened as a pancake. Wrath intermingled with Bob's heartache as he cradled the man, looked up to the heavens, sobbed, and shrieked, "YYYYYYYYEAS! I will kick his rock-hard cheeks!"

Bob ran to the other side of the tower to find the Moon right there, waiting for him. The General yanked his arms so hard into position that they sounded like he was cocking a pair of guns. The Moon was about to strike again, but he paused when he saw the General preparing a special attack. Bob spread his legs while he brought his hands close to his chest in middle-finger-strike position. Bob shrieked, "You've been a naughty adult!"

"And you're a depressed clown," the Moon quickly replied as he sardonically scrunched up his teensy-weensy face and self-importantly ran a gloved finger through his tiny toupee.

With a triumphant expression, Bob held the Moon's gaze in his rainbow eyes. In slow-motion, the Moon's expression fell into humiliation and terror. Bob uttered a phrase, crescendoing with and pausing after every syllable as the space rock pleaded, "No, no, no! Have mercy," and placed his hands over his heart. Meanwhile, a miniature Sun flowed from the General's middle fingertips as he progressed through his proclamation, which was, "Your mama."

The Moon shrieked, "NOOOOO!" as the deadly sphere of energy phased through his overlapped hands and cannon-balled through his heart. However, he sighed in relief, winked, and guffawed as he dropped his hands from his chest. "I have no mother," the Moon explained, before he push-kicked Bob. The General crashed into the populated skyscraper again and slammed through the ground floor, as well as twenty-one sub-levels.

In the dimly lit room, he rolled over onto his stomach to push himself up, but he collapsed; he hadn't landed on anyone this time. Since they didn't want to cross certain parents' threshold for fury, the news crews on this lowest floor switched to deep yellow filters as they raised the lights while Bob coughed up blood. The kids would think he had just choked on mustard; clearly it was too much too, since he was covered in the stuff, and he certainly was laying upon an expanding pool of it, they would reason. As coincidence would have it, he had crashed into a mega crate of super runny mustard, and he really was covered in the condiment, his mouth included.

His cuts were minor. Little white, adhesive, and x-shaped bandages were materializing (they looked like the ones in those slapstick Saturday morning cartoons), and they covered his scrapes.

Bob crawled forward, past the fresh holes above. The skyscraper fell upon him after the Moon crawled up the building and repeatedly jumped on it like a naughty child jumping on their bed.

Bob flash-backed to his father and their home in a bomb shelter, while a VHS anthology of injury prone yet immortal 'toons aired on their TV. The General was a child again and his father blew on his skinned shin before he applied ointment and bandages on his son's wound.

*Are you still alive, Poppa?* Bob wondered as he sobbed. He focused on his father as he clenched his teeth. He slowly raised the squished skyscraper upon his shoulders and outstretched arms, groaning with the endeavor. Every resident of the Earth cheered, including the people in the tower, as he stood, sweating and shaking, carrying the building. Bob looked around at the pancaked news crew and the destruction around him, and into the horrified eyes of the Moon who peered over the crater. The General locked eyes with his enemy, even as his daddy remained in his mind, while he slowly moved his hands and legs, one in front of the other. This way, the building eased back onto its foundation, but at a slight angle, as Bob left enough room for himself to climb up the hole. His determined, wrathful gaze into the Moon's disbelieving, regretful one continued as he arrived at ground level and stood inches away from his adversary's crouching face. Bob leapt with all his might into the Moon's nostril and arrived in his brain.

# Chapter III

## Unleashed!

As the General laid upon the Moon's orange-creamsicle-hued brain with his arms outstretched and legs closed, he experienced memories from his enemy.

\* \* \*

Gabriel Getty and his massive crew were of a microscopic race, with whitish-gray skin, oblong heads, and long tails that propelled them mightily through bodies of water. The race of slithies spontaneously came into existence a month ago, and among them was an impulse to invade our non-sentient moon.

Gabriel and his comrades arrived in phallic spaceships that easily broke through the moon's surface, effortlessly passed through the ebony clouds in the chandelier-lit sky, and broke apart on the frozen and champagne-pink ocean, whose numerous, towering gold-capped waves were suspended in animation.

Most of his team drowned amid shattered ice or died from the impact. Some of the similarly short natives, the Lunas, arrived from land on shrunken comets to adopt those who weren't grievously injured, while others entered on tiny sentient snowflakes to kill even the shipwrecked intruders who had minor injuries. Before either Luna faction of fetus-looking humanoids could accomplish their initial tasks, a war broke out between them, which promptly engulfed the multitude of Moon civilians, most of whose ideals fell somewhere in between the two camps.

As the war rapidly raged and the casualties gathered more civilians from either race than not, Gabriel dragged himself from his burning shipwreck and plunged into a massive hole in the ice behind him, where a comet and deceased snowflake floated. Some others followed his lead, but he had a head start, and only he had anticipated this war and trained for the grueling free-dive. He dove through the ocean and jetted to the moon's core; only he had planned to rule the moon by controlling it, rather than trying to colonize its people. He had also misled his crew about the moon's seasons.

Gabriel entered the core within minutes, and with magic incantations, everyone else within the rock blinked into non-existence, and he became the Moon.

* * *

Bob's consciousness entered upon a center seat in the lowermost tier of a brightly lit lecture hall. In the center of the room, on a massive podium that overlooked the auditorium seats around it, stood a human-sized being who looked like the tadpole's relative.

"Tonight, I will convert you into a devout loser," Gabriel's whispered proclamation journeyed throughout the auditorium.

"Go fuck yourself," Bob countered.

"That'd be a sin!" Gabriel shrieked as he slammed his palms on the lectern.

Gabriel regained his composure as he quietly projected, "You even have the audacity to not believe in any god, yet you can't prove that any of them don't exist."

"You don't believe in undetectable unicorns, yet you can't prove their non-existence."

"Have you ever wondered why Santa Clause, I, and so many others existed after you ran away from home? Your daddy knew what you were capable of, but somehow you managed to convince him to take you to the mall that day; sure, perhaps he was naturally loosening up to his natural personality. Nevertheless, you being a burden is beyond my point, which is this: you couldn't make gods exist, because they already do."

"I never stopped believing in God while being open to the reality of other gods, but what I no longer am is what my dear Poppa was in his fear and shame, and what you are in your lust for self-preservation and cruelty: a prejudicial dude who clings to a religion with doubts about your salvation, that can somehow be ever eventually secured by you. You're a mortal who thinks he is a god.

"You only exist to be defeated in such a humiliating fashion that others have a beautiful, good time."

"But you allowed me to commit genocide," Gabriel rhetorically replied in dawning horror.

"The greater the villain, the greater the hero must be," Bob dejectedly assured him as he bitterly cried, before the Moon blew him out through his nose.

The General dove through the massive tissue and landed on his feet. He punched toward the Moon, and the Moon countered by punching his adversary's fist while yelling, "'Sup!"

Agony detonated upon the Moon's fist as it snapped back. He retaliated by roundhouse kicking Bob through the slanted, broken skyscraper, which landed the General into an adjacent lobby of the opulent Smashing Hotel. The Moon charged into the high-ceilinged room and picked up Bob by the tassels of his pasties. He swung him round several times before releasing. The General crashed through the suites of a giant bipedal lizard, a towering monkey, a green humanoid behemoth, and the screenwriter. He slammed through the opposite exterior window, a kid's cotton candy, a flying saucer in the midst of abducting someone, and into the Nudists Don't Understand strip club. Bob grabbed a pole in mid-flight and swung himself around to sprint across the Moon who had charged after him. The General yelled, "I made a promise," as he marathon- kicked his enemy's hiney.

The Moon grimaced, and he crashed out of the strip joint as he tried to run away from Bob. "Doesn't your chest feel a bit chilly?" he inquired.

The General ceased his kicking, looked down, and saw that a pastie was missing. "My nippie!" he shouted as he placed a hand over it. Fortunately, the newscasters had the decency of pixelating it. Although, the nearby individuals who had seen his naked nippie blushed so rapidly and intensely that blood squirted from their noses. (Don't worry, they lived.)

"I'm sorry, I didn't mean for your pastie to come off!" the Moon genuinely apologized. "I thought it was secure," he followed up defensively.

The General sent a back-kick to the Moon, which landed him in an industrial city on the other side of the world. With a frustrated moan, the Sun fled to the opposite end of the planet, which caused a man to yawn, "Aw man, it feels like I just went to bed."

Meanwhile, the Sun replied, "You're telling me! I could have sworn that I was only gone an hour."

Meanwhile, a girl on the side where the Moon struggled to stand told her basketball mates, "Man, does time fly when you're having fun."

The General floated down in front of the cracked Moon a few minutes later, and the local reporters ran to his side.

Look, I didn't know he could fly either.

Anyways, the Moon had landed in a warehouse of nuclear warheads, and he gasped, "How did your heart handle the flight?"

"Not even the storyteller knows," the General confessed.

I nodded. After all, I'm just an observational fly who is transported to wherever a story takes me.

Bob smiled, retrieved a rocket launcher from the bottomless depths of his briefs, and pointed it at a warhead behind his adversary as he proclaimed, "Good night, Moon!"

Bob and the reporters walked away as the Moon was consumed by the atomic bombs' explosions, and time had the courtesy of enacting slow-motion upon the event. The scene faded to the title card, *Moondrop*.

The next scene faded into the cast with the crew, some of whom were religiously devout or atheists, and all of whom were human, as they bowed in front of the cameras (no one had died, nor was anyone injured). An animated rabbit in coveralls thumped to the front and announced, "The...the...the...the end, dudes!"

A mid-credits scene portrayed the creators deciding to make *Hell is on Earth* instead of *Moondrop*. An actor who was a war veteran performed in a war that the filmmakers started, and he became a casualty during a no-man's land sequence. *Hell is on Earth* won major awards from a prestigious organization, and the actor was also included in the ceremony's In Memoriam.

The post-credits scene incrementally revealed Santa Clause nearing the end of pasting the Moon back together. When the Moon's eyes snapped open, the scene cut to text that read, "General Bob Tom, Santa Clause, and the Moon will return."

# Book IV

# Cycles of the Phoenix

## The Aftermath

# Chapter I

## Book Signing

A twenty-four-year-old Indian American woman with a richly hued dying phoenix tattoo on one of her waxed arms, and a resurrecting one on the other, walked with her family from their home on a clear summer evening. A year and five months had passed since Dahlia Noelle lost part of her nose and some toes to frostbite; she was grateful that her endeavor to end her life didn't leave other marks nor impaired her mobility beyond a limp, but she was haunted by how close to death she arrived before she was found and how her abortion of the suicide attempt would have otherwise been too late.

Regardless, Dahlia was on a jittery high during July 9, 2003's approaching night because she had finally finished writing *Moondrop*, was pleased at the tale's absurdity, and was on her way to an authors' anthology novel signing across downtown with her loved ones.

Dahlia sat at a cafe table within the three story Montore Public Library, her place of occupation, and she shared a French Press brew with her mom and dad.

She checked her reflection in a compact. A dark brown woman with jewelry-lined ears, shoulder-length raven hair (which was tied in a half bun at the base of her head), almond-shaped, almost ebony eyes (which were lightly adorned by red and blue eye shadows), and thick eyelashes stared at her with a nervous, goofy grin. The prosthetic on her nose didn't look too shabby to her harsh self-standards, but she was feeling especially insecure about her yellowish smile. She snapped the mirror shut, sipped the library's dark-roast coffee, and held her *Cycles of the Phoenix* copy tightly in her hands, whose nails were painted with alternating jet-black and sparkly gold polish. Dahlia felt a special connection to this life-affirming, genre-diverse anthology on depression and anxiety, where the authors seemingly spoke directly to her, and revealed that some of them had received suicidal impulses that were strikingly similar to hers.

Dahlia and her family were an hour early, and the event had a significant crowd. She briefly got up and exchanged pleasantries with the individuals at the booth, some of the librarians who worked this night's shift, and several patrons. However, only the parents and some friends of the late co-author, Crystal Rosario, were among the authors there; they were there to represent Crystal's posthumously published portion of the anthology.

Thirty minutes passed from existence. A ninety-three-year-old woman entered with her husband, son, and grandchildren. After she situated herself at the book signing booth at the center of the library, Dahlia rose and greeted her and her family. The elder's name was Yuri Hara. Dahlia noticed that she looked a bit nervous, and Yuri confessed that she hadn't heard from Ray O'Sullivan, one of the co-authors, nor had anyone else she asked, but she said his daughter would arrive in about five minutes.

Seven minutes remained before the anthology signing's appointed time. Isabelle O'Sullivan, another of the anthology's literary artists, arrived with her mother, and panic overtook her when she saw that Ray wasn't there. She still hadn't heard from her father, the anti-suicide motivational speaker who had found overlooked stories from Yuri and her daughter (Kaya Hara) in a second-hand bookstore; Ray had helped bring *Cycles of the Phoenix* and this event into existence through his world-renowned publisher.

Isabelle's mother, Jiyah Ravati, had called the cops to search for him, telling them to check train stations and railroad crossings.

The event was delayed by thirty minutes before it was canceled without explanation. Dahlia's fearful conjecture was nourished by the expressions of the authors, especially Ray's family, and some of the attendees' whispered speculations.

Three days later, news outlets confirmed that Ray had committed suicide.

# Chapter II

## Kaya, I Love You

Several hours after Isabelle attended her father's funeral, she wearily tilted back until gravity pulled her to her double bed.

Isabelle reached for a copy of the December 1947 issue of an independent, defunct magazine that lay on her bedside table. She flipped to a tale by Yuri Hara that her father had wanted to save for *Cycles of the Phoenix*'s sequel, and Isabelle began to read it for the first time, this tale named "Kaya, I Love You."

\* \* \*

The land and sky rolled like a runaway train's wheel. A portion of the ground rapidly expanded and overtook the planetoid's floor. Aora Faust's soul was overstimulated from being violently unmoored from the walls of her body. Her mind intermittently managed to break the surface of an unconsciousness tsunami.

In her panic, Aora had entered free fall by teleporting seven miles into the sky and about five miles away from a surreal nightmare personified.

The walking horror teleported beneath Aora so suddenly and without spectacle that it was as if he was always there upon the misty rose hued beach, which bordered a placid lavender ocean. She tried to teleport again, but shock completed its arrest of her ability as the humanoid looked up. Deliriously, Aora tried to twist far away from the behemoth who had portals to universes within him, but paralysis seemed to infect all of her. Her friend, whose former appearance and aura brought comfort to her and everyone else, broke forth a pressurized, telepathic, high-pitched, and grief-stricken scream of countless souls, including his; this haunting explosion was carried over from miles away and detonated right in Aora's ears simultaneously, and his accompanying plea of "help me" could be deciphered alongside the wordless shout from the legion. Her eyes once again found Yuri, who was fighting alongside a hundred grieving individuals who were pressed tightly against one another. The melancholic individuals were trying to climb out of the Timeless Artist's eyes, which only revealed the clambering people within, covered in blood. Blood spilled down the towering life form's paralyzed body as hands broke through and grasped the perimeter of his eye sockets, but a force slammed them back down the impossible depths with such speed that they disappeared in moments with the screams. Aora plummeted after them, seconds later, into a pit with ebony walls and toward a pinprick of golden light that emanated far beneath.

As Aora careened through the Timeless Artist's haunted soul, memories of experiencing a new sensation from earlier that day flitted like directionless birds over the whirlwind of her panicked thoughts. The sensation of melancholy incrementally crushed her as if she were free diving to the ocean's lowest floor within seconds, and the approaching light was like that of a runaway train right before dawn, and the wind that rushed past her ears was that of a frantically whistling locomotive.

Aora was an indigo praying mantis who sensed when individuals upon The Tranquil Comet (her home planetoid) were experiencing steadfast, life-threatening depression, and she had the talent to teleport to them when the trust in their hearts was stronger than their fears and if their love for others was stronger than any cynicism. She often introduced herself as Day Yes Exophina-Machinatata, Deus Ex Machina for short, to these souls in-need, partly to lighten their spirits, and partly to drown her self-hatred when memories of self-perceived failure invaded her. Guilt was a poison that refused to leave or kill her completely; she routinely thought of the souls she didn't even have the opportunity to save, though she swore that if her powers were stronger, she could have preserved so many more lives and prevented numerous lifelong injuries from suicide attempts, including paralysis.

The Timeless Artist was an ageless being who lovingly created the souls (though not any of their powers) in this universe. He existed in many forms throughout the domain, yet the version that Aora and others in the galaxy could perceive without faith existed in a dimension that was home to him alone.

Aora had always perceived the Timeless Artist's empathy-induced melancholy as being as light and transient as a breeze. So confused terror arrived like a rogue wave without end when a detonation of debilitating depression from the Timeless Artist met her earlier that day.

Aora had seen the ground rush toward her before she realized that her legs had given way. When she lifted her face, she saw that the diverse beings she had been dancing with (without tiring) were experiencing it too, though not nearly as intensely, nor did they know the source. Aora sprinted away from the invading impulse to remain prostate and sleep forever. She had just enough faith that she wasn't too exhausted to teleport from her house to the Timeless Artist.

Aora arrived in his dimension and gently called the Timeless Artist by his personal name, even though she dared not look into his face. She felt her resistance to give up on him and flee, sink into a whirlpool and travel through a wormhole to the abyss when the Timeless Artist peered down and she saw them crawling in his eyes.

Aora finally plunged through the opaque golden circle of light that illuminated the end of the Timeless Artist's eye, and what smelled like decomposing meat and rusted copper that had been handled by sweaty fingers became so intense that it burst onto her taste buds and water-falled to her gut. She fell toward countless individuals of all ages who were mortally broken (some so much so that if someone happened upon them, they wouldn't be able to recognize them as bodies) yet some of their lives refused to depart. She plummeted through the heart of the familiar woman, an individual she met with Kaya during their adventure to the Timeless Artist nearly a year ago. Yuri was the summit of a mound of bodies that barely moved in their despondency, and Aora was transported to a dimension where Yuri could be perceived, though not interacted with.

* * *

Time did not make an exception for patience on behalf of Yuri and Kaya. Shock swiftly rose from dawn to noon upon Yuri's countenance after she opened her golden numbered, ebony-faced, and silver encased pocket watch. Kaya's expression reflected her mother's own as she gently set her floral mug of matcha tea upon the beverage speckled saucer.

The daughter's body language spoke of her chiding the impulse to grab her parent's hand and dash to the train station nearby. Kaya had surmised from the position of the sun and the slow, resolute descent of the timekeeper within the other's hand that her mother's worry was not one that was mixed with hope.

"I'm never going to make it to school, am I?" Kaya inquired, as she smoothed strands of her ebony-dyed hair over and behind her ear.

The thirty-year-old mom nodded a confirmation and an apology fluttered from her lips to her eight year old daughter, even as Kaya relayed that she wouldn't have traded the time that she shared with her in this place with perfect school attendance. Yuri absentmindedly rubbed tracks upon her face that were left by tears that weren't born out of the arrival of sorrow, but of catharsis; some of those tears had been her daughter's. Kaya stood up again and tenderly placed her smooth white hands within Yuri's own tan calloused ones as newly born tears fought to refill damp riverbeds and course new rivers upon the mother's makeup-adorned cheeks; Yuri nearly lost the battle as her daughter stroked the back of her mother's hands with her thumbs. Yuri and Kaya had finished confessing their depression and supplying affirmations to one another's souls through a story they improvised into existence; they really felt as if they had existed as royal adventurers in a magical world with fantastical beings, rather than a cozy cafe in Japan with fellow mortals.

That night, mother and daughter tightly held one another in an embrace anew after the restaurant's radio announced a historic devastation. Yuri gasped for breath and she sobbed with relief as she clutched Kaya (albeit not painfully tight) as if her daughter would vanish otherwise; they were safe, but Kaya would have lost her life if she had attended her first day at that new, faraway school.

"It's okay, Mom. I'm right here," Kaya consoled her mother. Yuri felt her daughter's heartbeat echo the call of her own. She focused on their hearts communicating in concert, the warmth of her daughter, and the gentle waves of Kaya's breaths meeting her rapid ones as she silently thanked God that her daughter was alive.

Kaya darted back and forth upon the ivory-white, fine-powdered beach and crystalline, sky-blue ocean on the day after as Yuri playfully chased her. The sand beneath their feet felt as warm as Kaya's exhale upon Yuri's cheek and the water was as cool as the breezes born from a flitting folding fan. Kaya slowed down enough for Yuri to swoop her in her arms, and her gleeful giggles and loose strands of white hair tickled her mother as she embraced her.

Kaya and Yuri lay next to one another on the beach, which they had to themselves, as the Sun neared the sky's summit. Yuri held her daughter's hand while they cried from improvised jokes that others may have chuckled at if they were feeling nice, and that either of them wouldn't find funny if that humor hadn't found them at the right place at the right time.

A cumulonimbus appeared on the horizon as the Sun sank midway between here and another side of the world. Its shape, as well as the color and angle of the sun rays upon it, made Yuri feel like she was on a small passenger ship within the most tempestuous portion of a super typhoon, and she wasn't sure why, but neither did she wish to know. Kaya fortunately squeezed her hand gently, but Yuri was disappointed when her daughter looked into her light brown eyes and gently said, "It's time to go home."

Yuri's former self wouldn't have wanted Kaya to stay up past her bedtime, and she would have been concerned about her daughter being out in the sun's rays for so long due to her albinism, though Kaya's custom swimwear reached her ankles, wrists, and neck; moreover, a fresh pair of dry gloves and socks, as well as a wide-brimmed hat, adorned her. Yet evidence of her daughter's sleepiness and injury were nonexistent. Furthermore, her daughter had a years-long wish to go to the beach during daytime, and Yuri's yearning to cherish as many moments with Kaya as possible had evolved, even when she had believed that its power was perfection.

Yuri beamed at her daughter as she lay in hospice as they reminisced about an event about half a decade ago from this moment.

Kaya had burst into their home office with her twenty one year old self, and she was over the moon. Her hair was a representation of chaos, while her mug was evidence of tea that had been filled to the brim and excitedly sipped by her, or had begun being drunk by a patch of floor during her jaunt from the kitchen. She held the beverage drenched cup in her left hand as she giddily plopped in front of her mother. Yuri giggled at her daughter, as she surmised, "You've figured out how to continue our story, haven't you?"

"Mhm!" Kaya affirmed as her purple eyes gleamed brighter. She reached under her sleeping garment and handed her mother

her quickly scribbled draft of their latest children's story that would have a happily ever after, but it wouldn't end just yet; they would strive to keep the narrative going forever if they could.

Kaya rubbed Yuri's arm tenderly yet firmly in the hospice room when they returned from the memory. "It's time to go home, Mama," Kaya whispered with tears in her eyes.

Yuri nodded, brushed her daughter's hair from her brow, and reached up to kiss her forehead as she fought her tears. "I know."

Yuri rose to her feet as she took Kaya's hand. Trembling, she followed her daughter outside of the door and found herself cradling an eleven-year-old Kaya as she hummed a lullaby to her daughter. Kaya had survived the nuclear blast in Hiroshima, and though she had overcome radiation sickness, she had scars from third degree burns, which stole her voice, and she was paralyzed from the neck down from the debris that had snapped her spine. She raised her eyes to her mother's, and Yuri heard her voice within her mind.

"It's time to go home, Mama," Kaya entreated.

Yuri broke down. "Please, let me at least have you like this."

"Live," Kaya pleaded. "Live for me, them, and yourself."

Yuri nodded and kissed her daughter's cheek. "Goodbye. Kaya, I love you."

"I love you too," her daughter responded as she wept in relief, brushed her mother's hair aside, and kissed her forehead. Kaya vanished in a blinding flash of light.

Yuri opened her eyes in her bedroom, as she finally accepted that her daughter had died six months ago, at eight years old.

Aora cheered for Yuri as she struggled to rise. Yuri's muscles had atrophied, but she also had to struggle with the grip of monsters that pinned her arms, chest, and legs for half a year (a few days after Kaya's death); entities that had also lulled her into creating blissful, fabricated memories, though their grips had been weakened by her determination. As the thirty-year-old Yuri continued to win the battle against the creatures that looked just like her, the individual who had been able to consistently help her awoke from a chair across the room. Fuyuko Imai, her lifelong best friend, rose to help her, but Yuri motioned for her to stop.

"I want to do this part by myself," Yuri wheezed. "You've already given so much. You helped me to return."

Yuri fell to the floor when she tried to stand as the demons around her desperately flashed painful memories of her widower father insinuating to her that she better abort any children because she would never be able to take care of them; he often reminded her, even if subtly, that it was her fault that his wife had died in childbirth.

Another memory exploded into being as Fuyuko rushed toward her, that of Yuri as a child whose clumsiness fed her father's hatred toward her, which fed her mistakes.

Though Yuri's father never physically assaulted her, he would verbally lead her to death's door many times, but Fuyuko (exhaustively clingy though that could be due to her fear of losing others' acceptance) had helped her to see her strength, and the beauty of her life, before her husband, son, and especially Kaya did too.

Still, she remembered the sense of despondency that plagued her when she became a mother. She had tried to connect with Daito, but she feared that he could perceive the melancholy in her soul despite her best efforts to hide it from him. She could sense that he became a bit afraid of her after she went into a debilitating postpartum depression when Kaya was born. She had felt as if she were failing her son, and she feared that she would fail her daughter too. Yet Kaya, a prodigy, only ever bequeathed love that was unaccompanied by fear.

Riku and Daito had striven to help her, even as Daito would spend moments avoiding her, and it broke her heart that her son would feel guilty about this. She understood that he was just a child and an individual who would always need time to heal from others' pain, even as she yearned for his presence. Similarly, Riku's frustration would slip through his resistance as he cared for her, even though his stress may have been due to him feeling inadequate at helping her. Fuyuko had attempted to lift her spirits, but she was going through her own struggles at the time.

Yet Kaya had always taken time to crawl toward her as soon as she could, her first word (unlike Daito's) was "Mommy," and she initiated cuddles with her mother as soon as she could walk, and she read her bedtime stories as soon as she could read; before then, and after, she would create fantastical tales (verbally and non-verbally) to cheer her up.

Yuri would later understand how Kaya developed depression from an intermingling of empathy, others' favored (if not jealous) treatment of her because of her skin tone, and a fear of failing others; Yuri would also discern how Kaya hid her melancholy while she masked her frustrations at anyone who would refuse optimism, even as she stubbornly loved them just the same.

Yuri allowed anxiety and self-loathing to pass over her during those rapid recollections as she latched onto recognizing her love for her family and Fuyuko. With that, she accepted her friend's help off the floor.

When Daito returned from school with his father, he dropped his textbooks and ran toward his mother in ecstasy. Even Riku, who had been mostly stoic since Kaya's death, sped toward his wife with tears in his eyes. The family held one another as they sobbed at the dinner table, as Fuyuko laid out a hot meal for them with gratitude in her heart.

* * *

Aora felt the Timeless Artist finally allowing himself to ease a bit. She exhaled with relief despite the cacophony of melancholy that hadn't decreased enough to stop tearing through her like a poisoned blade whose end was infinity. She sensed the Timeless Artist standing behind her. As she stood and turned around, she beheld him in the form of a jade praying mantis that was her height. Aora held him as she advised, "Empathy must be tempered by self-care, since denying empathy for ourselves, while embracing it for others, is a manifestation of self-hatred that places our perception of happiness upon others' shoulders. Then our faith in those who accept us is never satisfied, because we obsess over how we can ever be worthy of love.

"Furthermore, when we ceaselessly focus upon others' agonies, even going so far as to downplay their happiness by looking at it through a prism of pessimism, we debilitate ourselves; then what assistance can we possibly provide others?

"Moreover, the melancholy we suppress to deny its existence, or attempt to protect others from our pain (even to the point of imposing self-isolation), spreads until we either implode or explode. The irony of empathy without self-care is that it leads to self-paralysis or lashing out.

"When we set up boundaries of moderation, we not only allow ourselves to heal, we are able to sustainably help others as well."

Aora eased herself from the Timeless Artist as he apologized and thanked her. She clarified that he shouldn't give in to shame, and that depression wasn't something that could easily be waved away; it was something to handle day by day, though working toward and maintaining healthy boundaries would ease the struggle.

"It's time for me to go," Aora expressed. "I've given what I can give for now. I'm leaving because I love you, and I love myself. Yet I promise to visit, as I always do. I'll immediately alert others about what you're going through, but please don't hesitate to reach out to them too. Individuals cannot thrive alone. Each of us is a communal being, including yourself. Our souls are reflections of you."

With that, Aora encouragingly winked and teleported to her home.

\* \* \*

Isabelle arrived at the end of "Kaya, I Love You" and she held the magazine to her heart as she thought about how the Timeless Artist's trauma reflected her dad's own. She barely prevented fresh tears from breaking through the windows to her soul and chilly grief from causing her to shiver again. Isabelle placed the magazine in the drawer of her bedside table, turned off the lamp, breathed deeply, counted down from sets of ten seconds, and fell asleep.

Isabelle awoke a shade past twenty-four hours later and believed she had only slept a few minutes, until she saw the date on her phone. Isabelle fumbled for the lamp on her bedside table. When her eyes adjusted to the supernova that consumed the pitch darkness, she saw a meal that still gave off steam on her desk and a cup of water on the other side of her bed. Isabelle rose and reached for the note that was propped up on her stack of books.

Just in case you wake up and are hungry.

I'll wake you up tomorrow morning if you haven't returned from the Land of Dreams.

I was able to take another week off so we can spend more time together.

Love,
Mom

Isabelle whispered, "I love you, Mom," as she sat in her chair, thirstily gulped all the water, and ate one of her favorite meals, despite not having an appetite: dal tadka, basmati rice, and plain naan.

Isabelle finished her meal, wiped her hands with a moist towelette, and opened her blog. She wrote the following to her followers:

Dear Fellow Literary Adventurers,

We're crawling in the desert, our throats cracked as the hardpan. Occasionally dismembered shade flows over us, yet the quick comfort which it brings belongs not to the clouds but winged beasts who yearn to satiate their withered guts with the meat from our corpses. As we inch forward, we pray that the end to this wasteland which we see, wavering miles away, is not yet another illusion from the arid atmosphere.

Those of us who attain victory after each fall can grow weary from what seems like a war with a rapidly evolving virus; a storm which eventually collides like a tidal wave upon those lulls of contentment; an immortal hurricane that taunts as it periodically brings us into its center of tranquility...only to slam its wall of ferocity upon us again.

That experience is so exhausting that some are tempted to allow the Grim Reaper to carry them toward a freshly dug grave. So some become careful to not stray too far into the light again because it's a more horrifying experience to suddenly slip and plummet from such a great height than to remain in the canyon. Yet strife can still dig a chasm underneath the feet of those of us who refuse to climb. You see, hope isn't the enemy.

We all have battles to face every day, and if the actively self-righteous were to look within the souls of those whom they ridicule, then they'd see that many of us are victors who are fighting the best ways that we can, with all the energy that we have. So, let's not negatively compare ourselves to others. Though our outward accomplishments may seem less than what we did before, minuscule or even non-existent, they are truly equally exceptional as long as we try our best.

There is no such thing as a life without pain, but every day is worth living.

Love,
Isabelle O'Sullivan

Isabelle proceeded to click the email icon on her desktop computer. She casually glanced through the plethora of what she assumed to include condolences from fans, but one electronic letter stood out to her; it was from Yuri, and it was sent a few hours ago.

Dear Isabelle O'Sullivan,

Your father was an amazing soul, as you and your mom know better than anyone else.

I'm so sorry that I didn't attend your father's funeral. The truth is that I had managed to change my departure flight to tomorrow at 6:15 AM; I don't think you or your mom believed my desperate excuse, though you treated me with no less kindness.

Though I intended to join you and your mom for the funeral, I lost my resolve; I wouldn't have been able to comfort anyone during the funeral, and it would have been selfish of me to expect solace, much less so when I would be incapable of giving it at the time. I should have been honest about this right away.

By the way, there's a girl who is around your age who I think you'd get along wonderfully with, and her name is Dahlia Noelle. She works at the Montore Public Library. (Though I only interacted with her a couple of times during my trip here, I long ago learned to be in-tune with individuals' personalities.) I don't think you know each other since I saw no familiarity between you two on the night of the book signing, beyond what your fame bequeathed.

Anyway, Dahlia told me that she runs the library's book club meetings, which takes place from 8:00 to 10:00 on Saturday nights.

# Chapter III

## The End

Isabelle, Dahlia, and Milan charged toward an accelerating train in the desert. Milan was eight years old, while Dahlia was forty-one, and Isabelle was forty. Dahlia and Isabelle were nervous, but all three individuals were exuberant as they rode upon cheetahs; Dahlia's was sapphire with golden spots, Isabelle's was crimson with spots of silver, and Milan's was a rainbow-spotted ebony. As the family rode toward the ivory locomotive within Milan's unfolding story, Isabelle flash-backed to moments she shared with her spouse and their son.

\* \* \*

On Isabelle's first visit to the Montore Public Library's book club meeting, a few months after her father's suicide, she insisted that everyone there would not treat her as greater than them before she took off her disguise (a scarf, baseball cap, sunglasses, overcoat, full-length skirt, knee high socks, and boots) to reveal a medium brown skinned individual with long reddish-brown hair, jade irises, and a tattoo that adorned her left arm, which expressed "I am enough" in Hindi.

Isabelle subsequently pleaded to not be treated as if she were fragile, despite her recent trauma. The members barely tempered their glee and condolences (she was no stranger to happiness and sorrow being bedfellows) though she caught Dahlia blushing mightily and seemingly finding the floor quite interesting all of a sudden. Isabelle guessed, as she had when she met her on the night of the book signing, that Dahlia's admiration wasn't merely induced by her fame and her stories that Dahlia related to; Dahlia didn't react this intensely with the other authors who showed up that fateful night, months ago. Isabelle tried to temper her hope, since the few women and men she dated didn't match her personality.

Isabelle joined the big circle and expressed that she'd love to be a regular member of their club.

Dahlia picked up an extra copy of L. Frank Baum's *The Wonderful Wizard of Oz* for Isabelle and began to walk to her. When she was about halfway through her practically bouncing steps, Isabelle allowed her unconscious reactions to take over when she noticed Dahlia's foot getting caught in a looped lace of her sneaker. Isabelle dodged the flying book, while she simultaneously ran, hugged Dahlia, and descended into a controlled fall, just in time to prevent Dahlia from crashing into the mahogany carpet at full speed. Isabelle could feel Dahlia's panicked heartbeats echo into her adrenaline-spiked heart. Dahlia finally met Isabelle's eyes after she quickly let go and helped Isabelle up, and she broke her stare when she affectionately uttered, "Wow."

As some others checked if they were fine and were satisfied by the two woman's confirmations, Dahlia apologized, took off her shoes, and gathered the launched copy of *The Wizard of Oz* for Isabelle. To Dahlia, Isabelle said, "I'm thankful that you're not hurt."

Dahlia remembered the first night she made love to her wife since they had Milan (Isabelle conceived him through artificial insemination). She remembered admiring Isabelle's naked chest with giddiness.

"First time you've seen a topless woman?" Isabelle teased.

"No longer interested in seeing me naked again?" Dahlia playfully chided as she took off her bra and rapidly placed her hands over her chest.

"I find you more attractive day by day," Isabelle countered as she continued to undress.

Dahlia lowered her hands, kissed her wife deeply, and replied, "Same. Every day, I can't believe that I get more attractive."

Isabelle pretended to get angry, even as Dahlia needlessly stated that she was joking, and that she also found Isabelle more beautiful by the day.

Later on, they each placed their mouths to the other's ear and whispered, "I love you," as the other quietly orgasmed.

Despite their bout of lovemaking, the couple would have immediately put on nightgowns and rushed to baby Milan if he had cried; they had their auditory baby monitor on at full volume on their nightstand. After they stared at the device for a while as they cuddled, Dahlia turned to her wife and confessed, "I have something important to tell you."

Isabelle propped herself on her elbow with worry on her expression as she asked what it was.

Dahlia, with a dour expression that was betrayed by the laughter in her eyes, stated, "We're officially motherfuckers."

Milan recalled visiting a lady named Mrs. Hara and her family in Japan with his moms five years ago, which was two years before she died from old age. He was amazed at how youthful she appeared in-person for a ninety-eight-year-old. In the large home that she shared with her family, he had seen a few black and white photos of a young girl with whom he presumed to be younger versions of Mrs. Hara, her husband, and son. She enthusiastically told him about Kaya (who passed away due to what she vaguely referenced as a culmination of widespread dehumanization). Afterward, he expressed his belief that Kaya and he would have been friends if they had met as kids, to which Mrs. Hara gently squeezed his hand and stated, "I think so too."

\* \* \*

Milan, Dahlia, and Isabelle Noelle-O'Sullivan leveled with the speeding train and the mothers helped their son board it. Milan knew his moms were anxious around trains, though he didn't yet understand why, but they had agreed to accompany him on this story, so he held out his hand, and said, "It's okay. I'm right here."

With some trepidation, Dahlia grabbed her son's hand, boarded the otherwise unoccupied drivers' compartment, and joined her son in helping an anxious Isabelle inside the locomotive. The family thanked the cheetahs, and they blew kisses in return as the felines waved farewell.

Dahlia, caught in the moment, triumphantly began to shout, "Ffffffffuck yeah!" before Isabelle caught her attention with widened eyes. Dahlia, grateful that Isabelle prevented her from cussing in front of their kid, only made it to "fffff," before she improvised her way out of saying a curse word. She finished her phrase as "ffffaap yeah!" She realized her poor substitute for a swear word as Isabelle fought a battle of suppressing her laughter.

"Mommy, what does fap mean?" Milan questioned Dahlia.

"You know," Dahlia answered in a panic, "it's what birds do to fly." She rapidly waved her arms up and down as she elaborated, "Fap, fap, fap, fap!"

Isabelle burst out laughing.

Dahlia continued, "She's laughing due to shame because it's not a polite word to describe what birds do. The polite expression is "flap," rather than "fap."

"Nice save," Isabelle whispered to Dahlia as she overcame her giggles. She rubbed Dahlia's belly, which would soon grow rounder (Milan, who yearned for a sibling, would finally be getting one, and they would break the news to him at dinner), as Dahlia noticed the moon showing its face in the clear afternoon sky. She playfully shook a fist at the lunar rock as she blew a raspberry.

Karlo and Eleanor awoke from their naps. When they entered their living room, they saw their daughter, daughter-in-law, and grandson engaged in an imaginative adventure. Soon after, Jiyah entered with a platter of cookies that had just finished baking. After the family had their fill, Milan brought his grandparents into his story.

Jiyah boarded the train with the assistance of a phoenix, Karlo arrived on a giant speeding sloth, and Eleanor got there by running really fast.

The family observed the open desert ahead, and they carefully leaned out the compartment's open door to enjoy the warmth of the Sun's rays. One by one, they held one another, closed their eyes, and exhaled in contentment.

# Epilogue

## Sorrow and Bliss

Dahlia endured melancholy for the rest of her life, but she had learned to find happiness amid her sorrow too (she had also returned to therapy, and she incrementally braved honesty with her therapist this time).

Reality does not have Happily Ever Afters, and chasing after them only enhances misery. However, happiness can exist, even alongside depression. Though some days will be better than others, sorrow can be a companion (by way of others' help), rather than the leader of one's life.

# About the Author

C.A. Nicholas is an Asian-American, award-winning storyteller. His personality types are INFP and Enneagram 4.

He invites you to connect with him!

Website: canicholas.weebly.com

Email: canicholas.phoenix@gmail.com

Twitter: c_a_nicholas

Facebook: Charles.Avinash.Nicholas

# Also by C.A. Nicholas

### *Cycles of the Phoenix*

C.A. Nicholas's magnum opus symphony is about to begin, and he's reserved a seat for you. So come on in and I'll lead you to your place of honor as the house lights dim. Yes, your spot is beside the maestro as he teleports you and himself to various worlds! Diverse souls will befriend you there as they reveal the beauty of your life through their stories.

Made in United States
Orlando, FL
26 September 2023

37302885R00071